Island of Zarada

The Larimar Quest

by

Michele Evans

Island of Zarada: The Larimar Quest
by
Michele Evans

Cover Design by: JP Vilela

ISBN: 978-0-986294648

For my magikal butterfly, Mira.

PART 1

Miran's Inner Conflict

In the early promise of sunrise, two red orange discs rose from the east, blazing down on the cracked terrain. Morning crept along the island of Zarada, determined and impervious.

A furry bondo yawned, climbed up from its underground den, and wobbled to the watering hole, finding it still dry. Its black nose twitched in the stale air, smelling death. Emaciated bodies of dead and dying animals, winged and hoofed, lay scattered in and around the waterless hole, swarming with insects.

The bondo scanned the uneven crevices running along the pond bed, its small black eyes blinking slowly at the veiny channels, dark and deep. Wandering back to the edge of the forest, it licked paltry drops of dew that clung to wisps of brown grass protruding from the parched ground; all the water it would find until the next morning—if it could survive until then. A shadow passed along the ground and the bondo looked up to see enormous white wings sweeping across the sky.

Miran sat on her camion's back, dark hair whipping in the wind, eyes focused on the landscape below as she pulled the reins to the left, cutting close to the mountainside before aiming toward the field below. Making a smooth descent, she hit the ground running, bringing Cavalo to a halt at the barn where other young warriors were arriving.

Miran dismounted and walked Cavalo to his stall, unlatching the clasp. She gripped the steel handle and slid the heavy door open. In expectation of being fed, Cavalo lumbered to his feed box, letting out a deep and resonant "Reow!"

"That's my boy," Miran said, stroking his neck. She adored her camion, with his great big feline head and long white whiskers, pale pink nose, slanted grey eyes and magnificent white wings.

The feed supply was low the water well shallow. After scooping a small portion of food into the trough and pouring a slosh of water into his bucket, Miran said, "Sorry the portion's small, boy. We have to conserve."

It was summer season and the hottest one she could recall. She surveyed the grooming tools hanging on the wall. There was one brush that could smooth Cavalo's matted coat best when it got this tangled. Finding the one she was looking for, she lifted it off its hook and began the arduous task of brushing his fur. After passing the long thin silver teeth over his carmel colored fur, the knots began to give way and soon the brush glided easily. She continued onto the next section while Cavalo munched his breakfast.

Outside, the double suns of Zarada rose above the horizon. The heat was intensifying and Miran could feel the heat rise. After wiping the sweat from her face with a handkerchief, she removed her summer cloak and hung it on a peg. Her sheer blouse and knickers were light and comfortable, but she was still hot. She pulled her chestnut hair back, pinning it up off her neck.

The lack of rain over the last months had caused a drought. The situation was reaching a crisis; crops were stunted and withered, the stored food had become infected with a poisonous fungus. Water supplies were dwindling and there was no sign of rain. Only a string of sweltering days turning into weeks.

The High Council mandated a rationing program, so Miran's meals had been sparse lately. She complained when the bowl of grains had only amounted to a few mouthfuls that morning. She looked up at her mother, her stomach grumbling in protest. "I need more than that. I'm training today."

It pained Adean to deny food to her growing daughter. "I know darling, but that's all we're allowed. I've even given you mine."

Miran noticed her mother's plate was empty. "I'm sorry. I didn't realize."

As she secured Cavalo's saddle, she thought about another source of nutrition, one not found on the land but in the water—sea vegetables. *We have almost*

4

exhausted this year's harvest, she reflected. *The High Council must find a solution soon.*

As Miran finished securing Cavalo's saddle, her attention was diverted by a tapping sound. Cavalo's ears pricked up and he stopped chewing for a moment. Poking her head out, Miran spotted the source. A doken pecked at the base of the barn, where a nest of tasty insects scurried in and out of a sandy crevice.

There were many varieties of dokens on Zarada. This one had shiny emerald-green feathers and a glossy black head. Startled by Miran's appearance, it crouched, stretched its wings and flew off to perch in a nearby tree.

A voice called out, "Miran!"

Satrah appeared, her wavy black locks bouncing in the morning light, her female camion, Otho, alongside her. Otho had been ill the past few weeks and was not her usual frisky self.

"I'll be right out!" Miran called as she ducked back into the stall, emerging a moment later with Cavalo. The two camions greeted each other by placing their noses close together. Cavalo affectionately licked Otho on the forehead.

Other young warriors were converging in the field, chatting with one another beneath the trees where it was shady. Miranda noticed that Anay was the only one who hadn't arrived yet. There were plenty of days when she didn't show up at all.

Anay's mother, Selexi, was the daughter of the Sultana, and as a result Anay got away with many transgressions, including being absent whenever she felt like it.

"I wonder if she'll be here today," said Satrah, thinking of the same thing.

Miran shrugged. "Selexi doesn't like her to spend too much time with us."

"The High Council must be unhappy about that. They want us to form a united group. They're always going on about it. But it's okay if Anay breaks the rules. She's never held accountable."

Miran bristled. Thoughts of Anay always brought raw emotions to the surface. "We used to be friends. Maybe we could be again if—"

"—She's just mad because you were born early. She thinks you 'stole' the throne away from her. She needs to get over it."

It should have been a blessing but to Miran it felt like a curse. Selexi claimed that since her daughter was expected to have been born first, it was only right that Anay should be given the title despite the surprise birth order. The discretion stemmed from the law of inheritance that stated that every second generation a new warrior was crowned Sultana. The law read: *"The first girl born after the second new moon of the Autumn Season will inherit the throne."*

"Sometimes, I wish—" Miran started.

"What so you wish?" Satrah asked. "That you weren't born first? Don't even go there. I can't imagine having her for our Sultana. Well, I can imagine it and it's not a pretty picture."

"But she's a stronger warrior. She would make a better Sultana. Admit it. I'm no match for her."

Satrah was about to disagree. "Great. Here she comes."

Anay, full of haughty entitlement, rode up on a saddle adorned with expensive silver bangles. Her jet-black camion sharply swished his braided tail and hissed at Otho and Cavalo.

"What's the holdup?" Anay complained.

Satrah rolled her eyes. "What hold up?"

"We're right on schedule," Miran said.

"I thought we were late," Anay said impatiently.

"Things are not always what they seem," Miran said.

"Hmph," Anay said, clicking her tongue and continuing on.

Miran and Anay used to be friends. At the village school for young children, they were inseparable. The first time Selexi saw them laughing and playing together, she snatched her daughter away, scolding, "You shouldn't play with her kind." Selexi looked at Miran bitterly. "Your being named the next Sultana is just a technicality. The title really belongs to Anay. Everyone knows that."

Losing Anay's friendship was hard enough on its own, but what kept the wound fresh was the continual resentment and scorn which Miran felt acutely. It weakened her spirit, making her doubt herself at every turn. She didn't think she was worthy. She wasn't supposed to have been born first. It was an accidental birth order. Anay should be Sultana. Not her.

Satrah studied her friend's expression, "What are you thinking?"

"Is it wrong to want to be like everyone?"

"I suppose not. But—"

"—Then maybe I should give throne to Anay. It will solve the problem."

Satrah looked doubtful. "It will create new problems. Bigger problems."

Miran watched the last of the girls move away from the barn. "It's time to go."

They mounted their camions and trotted toward the open field.

The Warrior Academy

Miran had been given the role of leading the young warriors during training. The other girls had no hesitation in following her. She was unassuming and nonthreatening. In fact, some thought she was too passive. But they preferred her to the aggressive Anay, who sometimes took charge on her own. Assertion might be a desirable trait in a leader, but Anay was also mean-spirited.   During one sword training session, Anay had taken things too far.

She was paired with Arlia, a sickly girl who was timid and shy. "Lift up your sword and fight, weakling!" Anay commanded.

Arlia raised her sword tentatively only to be insulted further. "You must be slow, stupid or both!" Anay chided. Pretending to have trouble holding the sword steady, Anay mocked the poor girl, and finished the imitation with a fake faint.

Warrior Elder Madeek witnessed the whole thing and ordered Anay to run around the circuit until she dropped from exhaustion.

Miran surveyed the girls on their camions. Everyone was present. "Let's go!" she shouted. She kicked Cavalo and he broke into a run.

The others followed suit, and soon they were all charging across the field, leaving a haze of dust behind them. They gained enough speed to lift off the ground, their outstretched wings beating vigorously as they climbed higher and higher.

When Miran flew at these heights, her heart raced with excitement. The Trothe Mountain Range, which split the island into two, rose dramatically—earth tones contrasting with the blues and greens of the Topaz Sea below. On one side were the castle grounds and beyond that, the village. The other side housed the Warrior Training Academy and the Weapons House. A vast forest bordered the pristine beach, the treetops now more brown than green, the foliage sparse. The exhilarating ride, usually sweet and joyous, was tinged with angst. They could not survive another season without rain.

The Zaradians, strong and capable warriors, were a peaceful race, fighting only when necessary. Once, amongst some of the women, there had been discussion of discontinuing the warrior training. Mothers of the young warriors attended a meeting to discuss their daughters' future.

"It has been many years since we have fought in a war," Selexi remarked. "We are friends with all our neighbors. Those who are not our friends fear us. Why do we still need to train our daughters for fighting? It seems a waste of time to me."

"What if we're attacked?" asked Adean. "We must have warriors ready."

"We'll never be attacked," Selexi scoffed. "Our daughters would use their time more wisely learning other skills."

"We are feared because we are strong, it is our responsibility to stay strong," remarked Yivea, Satrah's mother. "All the women before us have been trained as Warriors. Our mothers and their mothers before them; It's our only defense if we were to have intruders with foul intentions."

"Besides, how do we know for sure that other islands aren't secretly training their own armies?" added Adean.

There were nods of agreement all around.

Selexi, angling to take over Zarada someday, thought a reduction in training might be an easy way to weaken the solidarity of the Zaradians but she quickly realized she would not win this argument. "You are all a bunch of foolish birds," she huffed.

Above and around the Academy spread thousands of acres of untamed wilderness. A year ago it had been a thriving ecosystem, bursting with life. Now it was a barren wasteland, peppered with dying plants and an array of odd weeds that could withstand the lack of rainfall. The animals that had thrived here before had either left in search of food and water or had perished.

They were approaching the secret passageway. Miran signaled to the group. The girls pulled their reigns and turned toward a low area of the mountain. They headed down toward what looked like a mass of tangled vines against solid rock. Usually lush and overgrown with plump green foliage, there now lay a tangle of dusty dead twigs. Miran pointed a wand at the area and chanted. The wand glowed and sent out a beam of light, creating an opening. They plunged in at full speed, the brittle overgrowth splintering into the air.

Miran, eyeing the landing spot, aimed Cavalo and hit the ground at a run. The rest followed and a storm of hooves pounded against the earth, studding the air with a storm of staccato beats as they galloped briskly around the graded curves that led to the Academy. They wove through the tunnel that threaded through the base of the mountain, wall sconces lighting the way.

They ascended another pathway, this one structured and lined with a metal archway. At the end was a doorway that led to the Academy. Miran passed her wand over the lock. It opened, and they entered.

Magik and Sword Training

The main purpose of The Academy was, like any school, to prepare the youth to be productive members of society. They studied all subjects with equal measure including history, language, music, art, science, magik, and mathematics. The Elders emphasized that along with these areas of study, warrior skills needed to be honed, so they would be able to defend themselves no matter what role they played in daily life. Everyone on the island was trained to be a warrior.

The Magik Training Hall had walls and ceiling made of rock. The room had twenty-four tables set up in eight rows, on which the Magik Arts were learned and practiced.

Magik was a dangerous undertaking. It could do much good, but if misused, could create undesirable results and cause irreparable damage. There were multiple levels of proficiency and varying intensities of the wand to learn. Miran's group was at an intermediate level, working on perfecting the manifestation of objects. Tutors assisted the students and a wand keeper kept meticulous records of the wands signed out at the beginning of every class and made sure they were returned at the end.

Everyone on the island was capable of invoking basic magik spells and each household was equipped with a beginner level magik wand, kept under lock and key, to be used only for emergencies. Magik was strictly forbidden without permission except for certain situations. There were laws in place to keep the islanders from turning to magik for any reason. That would be chaos.

Magik training was followed by academic study comprised of history, science, math and literature. The girls complained of thirst. They were given small sips of water at scheduled points during the day. They broke for a midday meal, which these days were more of a snack than the hearty fare they were used to.

Their last class was Sword Discipline. The girls went outside to the training arena, filing into six lines. Madeek, Head Warrior Elder, stood on a platform at the front of the formation.

Madeek had fought and won many battles for Zarada. Large boned, with a sinewy body, she had the gait of a predator. A jagged beet-red scar started at the bottom of her right eye and traveled down in a diagonal line to the top of her upper lip. Her sharp grey eyes, luminous in the sunlight, pierced like cold metal, missing nothing. Coarse white hair gave away her advancing age but her body was lithe as a youth. Using

14

her robust lungs, she shouted out her first command of the day. "Swords up!"

The girls held their swords with two hands, the knotty wooden handle clasped with a short cylindrical steel band. Swirling pink light shot up around the blade, tapering to a point. In unison with the others, Miran grasped her weapon and held it up.

Madeek paced back and forth like a caged animal, stomping out a fierce rhythm. "Swords down!" she cried.

The girls flashed their swords to the ground in a downward motion and waited.

Madeek continued to pace as she barked, "We use two swords; the ones in your hands, which transform, and the ones that are locked away, which can kill. As a peaceful society, we practice the art of self-defense. May the day never come when we must use the swords of destruction against a violent intruder." Madeek scanned the girls' faces. "But if that day ever comes, we are prepared to fight—!" She raised her fist, already victorious. "—and win!"

She bore her steely gaze into the eyes of each girl, testing their mettle. "Raise up!" she commanded.

The girls turned to the right, raising their swords to the sky.

"Ready!" cried Madeek.

In perfect unison the weapons blazed up into ready position.

Madeek jumped and performed a dizzying flip, kicking outward in midair, away from the platform, landing squarely with two feet on the ground. Her gruff voice echoed loudly as she bellowed, "AZUKE, SHARNUE, LUKAH!"

The girls performed three maneuvers: a complex flip, a dizzying turn and several quick sword slices. The air buzzed with the sound of quickening blades. Madeek watched for accurate technique and smoothness during transitions. When the moves were completed, the girls stood still.

"Ready!" Madeek cried.

The girls picked up their shields, turned to face each other in pairs and held their swords up in ready position.

"SPAR!" Madeek cried.

The lights from the swords danced, jumped and spun in a frenzy as the sparring ensued. The real test had begun.

Anay, a tower of strength, had just attained Supreme Warrior status. With her agile movements and flawless technique, she was feared and respected by the others. She easily out jumped, out spun and out witted her opponents in speed, cunning and skill. In the flurry of light that the swords created, hers could be picked out as the swiftest.

Madeek observed Anay's capability with pride, but the pride was tainted. She didn't like Anay's ruthless tendencies. Power without discrimination led to corruption and cruelty.

She wasn't as impressed with Miran's sword work. What stood out in Miran's style was not so much a lack of ability as a lack of desire. She exhibited grace without drive, competence without passion, skill without focus. But what Miran did have was a pure heart and that was worth more than all the fighting prowess that Anay possessed.

Today, Miran's partner was Satrah whose skills were not to be discounted. Satrah was quick moving, steady and focused. She was trying to engage her opponent, but Miran's mind seemed to be elsewhere.

Miran defended herself well enough against Satrah's attacks, but it was more play than anything for her. She just didn't take it seriously. She lost her concentration for a moment and caught a glimpse of Anay.

Miran was so amazed by Anay's expertise, she didn't realize Satrah's sword had touched her shoulder—and now she was encased in a field of swirling light, paralyzed. The sparring was over. Half the girls were frozen in a cocoon of pink light.

"Transform!" commanded Madeek.

One by one, each imprisoned girl was changed by the whim of their victor; one was turned into a tree, another a table and still another a cup of tea.

Satrah smiled playfully at Miran, who twinkled back with her eyes. Satrah knew what Miran liked best to be transformed into. She recited a spell in the old tongue and Miran was changed into an iridescent blue doken. Satrah laughed as Miran promptly squawked and flew away.

Reluctant Future Sultana

Alone under the umbrella of an endless blue sky, Miran felt the layers of worry peel away and dissolve into nothing. She adjusted her wings to the wind's subtle currents, enjoying the perfection of balance and the lightness of her doken body. Gliding smoothly, she swooped up and down, toying with the salty breeze. As she approached the rocky mountainside, she tilted her wings to avoid the rough edges.

Then the warning signs set in; the loss of wing power, the dulling of her senses. Realizing she was about to transform back, she turned and headed for home, soaring over the rocky terrain, passing over the forest that led to her cottage made of wood and stone.

She spotted the crude sturdy roof, the picture windows and red front door. Aiming for a tree, she gripped one of its thick branches with her talons and folded her wings. Her mother, was in the garden patch, which had slowly turned from promising green shoots into a dusty collection of dried sprigs.

"Squawk!" announced Miran, cocking her head.

Adean glanced up. "Oh, dear, not again."

Miran descended to a shady spot next to her mother, where she lay down, remainging still for some time. Then she convulsed, morphing into a series of unidentifiable shapes before her original form emerged.

Adean set down her spade and sighed. She reached over and caressed her daughter's cheek. "Miran. Sweetheart, wake up now."

Miran opened her eyes. Her throat was parched. "Hi, Mom," she croaked.

Adean ran her fingers over her daughter's forehead, smoothing away the mess of hair. "What about Cavalo?" she asked.

"Satrah will take him back to the barn."

Adean turned her attention back to the garden where withered vegetables hung from dry stalks. Frustration lined her face. "Look at these plants. They're just about dead. What are we going to do?"

"How am I supposed to know?" Miran answered, standing. "The whole island is dying. Soon we'll be dead too I imagine."

"Miran! Really. It's not a joke."

Freya, Miran's younger sister, came running out. "Mommy, I can't find my doll."

Adean gave up on the garden. "I'm coming in now. There's nothing more I can do here."

Miran started toward the door. Adean touched her arm. "Look at me."

Miran reluctantly met her mother's gaze.

"You are going to be our next leader."

"So?"

"So—people are going to look to you for solutions to all kinds of issues. You will need to be strong enough to fight your opponents…and win. You have to *want* to win. The Sultana has to be a Supreme Warrior in order to inspire the rest of us. If there's ever a war, you may have to fight for your life and the lives of everyone on Zarada. Even if you don't fight yourself, there will be other battles—of the mind and the heart. You don't know what challenges await you, so you need to ready. Others will look to you for answers. Lives will be at stake. Your decisions will determine outcomes."

Miran didn't like what she was hearing. At the same time it was exactly what she wanted to talk about. She went inside. "Why do *I* have to be the one with all the answers? The High Council, The Brotherhood and the Priestesses know more than I do. They can run everything without my help. They'll see right away that I don't have anything to contribute. I'm just a kid and honestly, I want it to stay that way. Let them figure it out."

Greet and Vita, their fairy housekeepers, had been busy polishing the doorknob and were almost pushed into the wall by the brisk opening of the door.

"Oh!" Greet exclaimed.

"Sorry!" cried Adean. "Are you okay?"

"We have wings!" squealed Greet.

"That's what they're there for!" added Vita.

Freya giggled along with them.

21

Normally, Adean joined in the fairies' fun, but she wasn't in the mood. She continued her line of conversation as she followed Miran into her bedroom. "They *will* want to hear you and you'd better have something valuable to say, or you'll lose their respect. They will be patient with you at first because you are so young. But they won't tolerate foolishness."

Miran was tired of the subject. "Why do I have to do it? I never asked to be Sultana. I don't want to be the leader, and I don't want to have anything to do with war. I just want to eat." In an attempt to escape, she went to the kitchen in the vain hope that there would be something there to fill her empty stomach.

Adean came in behind her. Together they looked at the empty cupboards. Adean, full of despair, swallowed hard with thirst. "Do you ever think about anyone other than yourself?"

Miran closed her eyes. Deep down she loved her mother.

Adean took a deep breath, her voice dropping almost to a whisper. "I hope you never have to lead us in times of conflict. But you must understand that even though the High Council and Priestesses may have more experience, you will still be our Sultana. If you don't lead, you will be voted out. If that happens, Anay will replace you. You don't want that, do you?"

Miran did want that, but she wasn't ready to let her mother know. It would only upset her. Instead she gave Adean a hug and went to her room. Sitting on the edge of her bed, she thought some more. *Perhaps the way to solve this is to go through with the coronation but be a poor Sultana. Then Selexi and Anay can take over and I will be free of the grip of its hold on my life.*

Daemons and Red Larimar Stones

Miran passed a shell brush through her long chestnut hair, her deep blue eyes tracking the motion of the brush in the mirror. Candles threw patterns of light and shadow on the walls, their golden flames dancing. Outside the window, two full moons rose, casting a glow onto the objects in Miran's room—her bed, her dresser and the vanity table where her favorite family photos were arranged. The pictures, set in ancient hand carved wooden frames or in pounded bronze casings gave her comfort.

She looked at the figures in the pictures, the unflinching faces that stared back at her—silent mouths and steady expressions frozen in time. There was the one of her father posing on the beach. Next to it was a charming shot of Freya in the garden, holding bounty from the harvest—a year when the fruits and vegetables had been ripe and bursting with life.

Then there was the one she loved most of all—the five of them having a picnic by the river; her mother laughing, her father beside her holding Freya in his lap. Miran sitting with her knees pulled up under her, all smiles for the camera and her grandmother, Galanee, her arm wrapped around Miran's shoulders.

She gazed at the photo of Grideon, her true love, the one she had chosen to marry when she became Sultana.

Her eyes settled on a picture framed by fine brass inlaid with opal stones, arranged in a mosaic. It was Galanee when she was a young warrior. She stood at the bow of a ship, her hair whipped and tossed by the wind. Her face was tilted upward, her eyes gazing out to a point far off in the distance. A pewter charm lay against her chest; the figure of the Rain Goddess, a gleaming red larimar stone inlaid at the heart.

Miran admired her grandmother's brazen expression. Her attention moved to the pendant and she was pulled in, transported into the world of the picture…

Miran, 5 years old, feels herself being lifted up. Bitter winds bite against her face, her cheeks feel numb. She feels ruddy hands lift her up, place her in a lap and looks up to see it's her grandmother.

Galanee feeds her sweets; sings to her.

"Mabu, where are we?"

"You finally found me. I have been waiting so long. I knew you would come. Here, have another." She holds out a piece of pink candy.

Miran takes it and pops the sticky ball in her mouth, savoring the sugary flavor.

*"But where are we going?" Miran feels herself
slipping away.*

"Follow me," Galanee says, floating off.

"Don't leave me, Mabu."

*Galanee fades, but her voice is clear. "I'm just over
here. Come along."*

*Miran tries to follow the voice, but
the floor falls out from under her. The fog rolls in,
she can't see anything but grey mist. She falls into a
puddle. Wetness soaks her cloak and the cold water
finds her knees. She's held there as if by a weight.
Unable to rise, she lifts her face, grimacing, eyes wide,
searching.*

"Mabu, where are you? Come back!"

Miran jolted back into the room. She found herself
on the floor, breathless, as if she had run for hours.
Adean was next to her, "Miran, are you all right?"

"I must have collapsed."

"Another one of those visions?" Adean asked.

Miran nodded, clutching her mother in the
darkness. "Is she dead?"

"I don't know. Probably."

"Tell me about the daemons again."

"Oh, Miran, you don't need to have those horrible
images floating in your head. It's just going to make it
worse."

"Tell me about them."

26

Adean relented. "The daemons live on the summit of Saron. They guard the red larimar stones that we need to make rain. Anyone who is caught trying to take the stones is killed and turned into one of them."

"When did she go there last?"

"You were ten."

"Do you think she's a daemon now?"

"I hope not."

"Maybe she'll come back someday."

"Maybe. You need to sleep now. I'll take you to bed."

Miran let her mother help her get into bed and cover her with the blankets. As the soft light of the moons lulled her to sleep, she wondered if her dear, precious Mabu was out there, somewhere, thinking of her, too.

Astrielle Prepares

The bondo, his matted brown fur swathed in dirt, emerged from under cracked leaves as dawn broke in the Fairy Forest. Shards of shimmering gold sliced down between the branches and silhouettes of dokens swooped in and out of the treetops as they cried to the rising radiant suns. A hungry nocturnal tiger mouse and her malnourished young pups settled into their stone cave to doze and keep cool throughout the scorching day.

The bondo shook the dirt loose with the little energy he had left, his thinning frame weakened by acute hunger. He sniffed for the puce worms and black insects that made up his breakfast. After an extended search, he dug one up and was about to bite into it when another bondo jumped in front of him, threatening to devour the prize. He bared his fangs and swiftly attacked, sinking his teeth into the rival's neck until it struggled no more.

A whirring sound seeped down from the treetops— the unmistakable purr of fairy wings amidst a symphony of giggling and cajoling. Their shimmering wings zoomed here and there, trails of light painting sparkling

More fairies flitted out of homes built into the trunks and limbs of ancient trees. Their miniature domiciles were furnished with everything necessary for living; tiny curtains, minikin stoves, and beds no larger than a shoe.

Astrielle stirred under her coverlet as the sounds of morning trickled through her peephole windows. A bell hanging from her front door was ringing. It roused her from slumber. Realizing she had company, her eyes fluttered open. She knew who it was; Pongo, coming to pick her up for another big day and the last one they had to get ready for the Sultana's visit.

Pongo let himself in, flying from one window to another, briskly pulling back the floral curtains. "Astrielle," he sang. "Time to rise and shine."

Astrielle sat up and stretched her wings. "Mmmm, all right!"

get lost in dreamland pretty fairy?" He smoothed his hair   and straightened his shirt. "Oh, my, my new pants got a wrinkle."

"All the work this week for the Sultana's visit has made my eyes thick with sleeping dust." Astrielle waved her hand over her eyes and the dust dispersed in a sparkle. Flapping her wings, she lifted out of bed and in a dazzling, spinning flash, she whirled out of her nightgown and into her day clothes.

"Well, this is our last day to get ready, so put a flip in your zoom and a zing in your fling." Pongo waved his hand to the door. "Get what I mean?"

Astrielle giggled. She was eager to finish the decorations. She poured water into her kettle. "Let me have a cup of tea first, I think there's enough water."

Resigned to waiting, Pongo took a seat. "Don't worry. The Sultana will solve this. We'll have rain soon, somehow."

"But she's very ill, Pongo. She's old and dying and will leave us soon."

"How do you know that?"

"I saw her."

"You? When? How? Why?"

Astrielle giggled.

"And, what for?"

"Oh, Pongo! Stop!" She giggled. The teakettle whistled in harmony with Astrielle's peals of laughter. She lifted it off the burner and poured the steaming water into a cup filled with crushed berry tea leaves. "Yes. Last season. As she was out walking with her cane. Because I was visiting with my friends in the castle."

Pongo applauded her thorough reply. "Very good."

Astrielle took a sip of tea. "She looked deathly ill at that time. I'm surprised she's well enough to come."

"She can't resist us."

"True. She has always had a soft spot for fairies. I think we're going to have our problem solved not by her, but the next Sultana."

"Who is that going to be again? I forget her name. Miria? Matina? M—"

"Miran. She's very young and that means she will have new ideas."

"I will miss our Sultana Henrit."

"Indeed." Astrielle downed the last of her tea.

Pongo bent one leg, opened the little door and extended his arm toward Astrielle. "Shall we?"

Astrielle took his hand and he twirled her gracefully out the door. They leapt off her porch to join the throng of fairies making haste to the fairy courtyard where final preparations were already well underway.

The Sultana's Failing Health

Sultana Henrit had ruled a long time, almost her entire life. Although her mental capacities were still as sharp as a pin, she grew weaker, many days incapable of fulfilling her duties. Heggor the Healer had kept the degenerative process at bay as long as she could. But in order for the treatment to work, the fibers in the body had to be resilient enough to respond to the light energy pulse and compounds in the tinctures. The Sultana's fibers had been revived so many times, they had completely worn out, never to become pliant again. Her body was being consumed by disease and death was approaching.

Aching from head to toe, she lay in her bed, propped up by burgundy velvet pillows. Her attendant, Raina, was briefing her on the upcoming trip to the Fairy Forest.

"We leave tomorrow, midday," she said as she leafed through a set of papers, making sure she'd gone over the important points. "Everything's ready for your visit…" She paused. "That is, if you're sure you're up to it."

The Sultana wasn't sure if she was up to it, but she was resolved to go. "Of course I am."

Fairies had been friends of the Zaradians from the beginning, as far back as Undua, the Sultana who settled them on the island. Every family housed two or three fairies, employing them as companions or housekeepers. They took the positions voluntarily and were amply compensated for their services. Fairies were nice to have around. With their charm and easy laughter, they became part of the family, frequently living out their lives in the care of those who they had taken care of.

"I love the fairies so very much, you know," sighed the Sultana. "Can you believe I have never had a disagreement with any of them? Not one. They have to be the most agreeable darlings I've ever known."

The Sultana regarded the two fairies at her side, Nika and Tika, twins. They had been with her for many years, turning old and grey right along with her. They smiled at her kind words.

The Sultana sat up a bit, energized by memories of the past. "When I was only a small child, my mother left me alone in the meadow for a few minutes while she went back to our dwelling for a basket she'd forgotten. I became hot and sought the shade of the nearby forest. I was familiar with the fairies who lived with us but knew nothing of the multitude that dwelt in the trees."

"Shortly after I entered the forest, I heard the strangest sounds—humming and buzzing and waterfalls of laughter. I was mesmerized by trails of light that wove in circles around me. I tried to see what they were, but they zoomed by so rapidly, I couldn't make them out. Then one hovered right in front of me and I said, 'You're not *my* fairy.' She laughed and asked if I were lost. Then she took me back to the meadow where my mother was calling for me."

The Sultana was happy to talk of such things, but it made her tired, short of breath. "So you see, I've always had a special place in my heart for the fairies. They fit in the palm of your hand but have hearts the size of mountains—" She stretched her arms out to illustrate the size of fairies' hearts but was seized by a fit of coughing.

Nika and Tika rushed over.

"Rest now, Sultana," soothed Tika.

"Don't talk anymore," added Nika.

Raina poured a pool of sapphire syrup into a wooden spoon and brought it to the Sultana's lips. The coughing subsided and she sunk back into the softness of the pillows, letting the soothing tincture bring her sleep.

Fairies Shouldn't Fly at Night

Astrielle yawned. It had been a long day laboring in the courtyard. She, along with thousands of other fairies, had spent countless hours weaving and winding a string of delicate white garlands through the branches of the outdoor theatre where the Sultana could enjoy their fragrance and beauty. They usually used the fuchsia trumpet flowers. But only one flower had blossomed this year—a drought resistant, less fragrant bloom that didn't have quite the same elegance but turned out nicer than they had expected.

The suns descended as the fairies finished their handiwork; pink and orange swirls bled into indigo as the horizon folded into dusk. Normally talkative and playful, these tired fairies were bleary eyed and silent. Along with the hard work, the rationing of food and water made them uncharacteristically listless. Rehearsals ended, the musicians packed up their instruments, while dancers and acrobats shimmied off the stage.

The supervisor stretched his arms and rubbed his eyes. Then in an effort to muster up some good cheer, he flew backwards to observe the effect of the long day of toiling. "You've done a lovely job everyone!" He flipped a switch.

They all looked up to see the effect of their endeavors. The paper-thin white blooms lacing through the trees formed an entrancing, lilting pattern that covered the theater and beyond. With the lights on, the flowers looked like they were glowing from the inside out.

The sight sparked a little energy back into the group.

"Look at that!" said one.

"Wondrous!" said another.

"All right, you can go home now," said the supervisor. The fairies congratulated one another, said their goodbyes and fluttered themselves into the darkening sky.

Astrielle searched around for Pongo. He had been working with the performers, but now he was nowhere to be seen. Assuming he had left already, she headed home.

She was more tired than she realized and found it difficult staying awake in the dying light. Sleep-flying was a perilous enterprise for fairies. Easy to slip into, it was a danger to be avoided at all costs. She caught herself nodding off a couple of times and told herself she must not fall asleep. But fall asleep she did, and quickly.

She slowly descended, her wings folding in repose. Reaching the ground, she was lucky to have landed in something soft, but she had the misfortune of landing in the gluey, sticky web of a carnivorous orak. And that orak, who had been in a kind of predatory half-slumber known only to oraks, felt the welcome vibration of dinner arriving.

Astrielle wasn't the least bit disturbed by the fall. She sighed gently, snuggling into the blanket of softness, a smile curling at the corners of her mouth as she surrendered to peaceful oblivion.

A few feet away, in its underground nest, the red eyes of the orak flicked open. Lengthening its legs, its body raised up and it began grooming its mandibles in preparation for a long awaited meal.

Trapped

The orak secreted a thin layer of venom from the tips of its fangs. When a sufficient amount had coated the razor sharp points, it lifted its two front legs and used them to polish the fangs in a flurry of swift strokes. When that was done, it raised its antennae into the air to sense the rapid rhythm of blood coursing through Astrielle's body. Having dined on fairies before, it recognized the beat. It also sensed something else—the vibration of something approaching from off in the distance—something much larger than itself.

From the depth of the forest, a faint melody wove its way through the air. It was the voice of Miran, who sang as she rode Cavalo through the dusk, her voice filling the forest with an old island strain.

Oh Mother Moons
Oh Father Suns
Oh Terra life
If the truth be known,
Then the way is light.
And I will use my might
To protect my home.

Her three pet ninxes—four legged animals with able snouts and digging paws—trotted alongside her. She had taken them here to dig up wild roots and now her saddlebags were full of these savory morsels. They were on the small side and a little wrinkled, but they would have to do. She ambled along, enjoying the peace of the forest she loved so well, but her tranquility was not to last.

Astrielle's eyes fluttered open. At first she didn't know where she was. Then she realized what had happened. A smile drifted across her lips as she mused at her folly. But when she tried to get up and couldn't, she panicked. Her resting place was no ordinary bed of leaves. It was the terrible trap of a deadly orak. Fear faded her smile and chilled her to the bone.

She struggled against the viscous substance but it was impossible to pull away from the gluey web. She knew exactly what was coming; a gruesome death involving fangs, an ending all fairies feared and which many succumbed to. Any movement might bring her killer sooner, but she had to take the risk. There was no other choice. She cried out as loudly as her little voice could go. "Help! Help! Anybody, help, please!"

Miran heard something coming from deep in the forest. It was faint yet clear and high-pitched. She brought Cavalo to a halt. A ninx rubbed up against Cavalo's leg, provoking an affectionate "Reow."

"Quiet, boy," she whispered, listening closely. "I know what that is—a fairy! In distress!" She prompted Cavalo and he broke into a gallop.

The orak made its way through the nest and up toward Astrielle.

Moonlight filtered across the edge of the opening. Astrielle saw the orak's shadow and fear struck her heart. "Help!" she cried out again.

Suddenly, the ground began to quake. The heavy trampling increased in intensity, making the orak hesitate. Astrielle began to hope.

Miran called out, "Little fairy, hold on! I'm coming!"

"Please!" Astrielle answered. "Hurry!"

Miran sped past the trees, following the small voice. "Where are you, fairy?!"

"Over here!" Astrielle answered. "Here I am!" Astrielle saw the blur of Cavalo's hooves. *What luck! A young warrior!* "Down here!" she exclaimed.

"There you are," Miran said, jumping off Cavalo. "I'm here now, don't worry." She placed her hands around Astrielle's waist and pulled. The sinewy web stretched but would not break.

"Oh it's no use!" sobbed the little fairy.

Miran pulled harder and the web elongated, stretching thin and taut. But still it would not break, holding fast to the tree roots it was attached to.

The orak poked its head up through the hole, surveying the situation. It didn't like competition and was hesitant to reveal itself to such a large creature.

"Look!" cried Astrielle, her eyes fixed on the orak's menacing stare. "There's the monster that made this web!"

The orak jumped toward them. Miran pulled to the left, just out of reach of the fangs. The lithe predator landed on the other side, confused, but then understood it had missed its mark. It turned around and eyed its lost prey.

Miran pulled out her dagger.

With all her strength, she strained to bring Astrielle toward her, pulling the web as hard as she could and began sawing through the tough fibers with the dagger.

The orak paused, momentarily mesmerized by the rapid movement until hunger snapped it out of its reverie. With tiny forward movements, it drew closer, positioning itself for a strike.

Miran stopped sawing to take a stab at it, but it dodged the attack and scurried into a crevice in a rock. She continued to cut at the web. When she was down to the last strands, the orak jumped out from its hiding place and raced up to snatch its prize. The final string of web snapped apart just as Miran pulled Astrielle out of reach.

Astrielle was safe but the orak's sharp fangs sunk into the flesh of Miran's hand. "Ooow!!" she cried. The pain shot up her arm as the poison entered her bloodstream. Her vision blurred and the forest spun around her. Numbness started at the top of her wrist and traveled all the way down to the tips of her fingers. Feeling faint, she lost her grip on Astrielle and stumbled, falling to the ground. She blinked over and over, but everything was fuzzy. And then all went black.

"Aaaah!" Astrielle cried, landing hard on her right wing. She tried to fly but couldn't lift off, the wing was too damaged. She broke into a run, wisps of web trailing behind her, creating a perfect target for the orak. It scurried after her on its spindly legs until it caught up, pulled her into its grip and sank its fangs into her neck.

Miran's eyes blinked open, her vision restoring enough to see the orak taking Astrielle toward its nest. Fighting the effects of the poison, she rose to her knees and raised her dagger with both hands, sweat dripping down the side of her face. *I must be exact. There!* She brought the dagger down swiftly, and—*crack!*—pierced through the orak's brittle abdomen.

Astrielle was unconscious, her body limp. Miran gently lifted the fairy and was relieved to feel a heartbeat, brisk and steady. She placed Astrielle in the front pocket of her cloak, mounted Cavalo and headed for home.

Astrielle's Discovery

In the quiet stillness of dawn's blue glow, Astrielle slept peacefully in the silky interior of a hand carved wooden jewelry box. Miran had emptied it the night before, removing necklaces and rings before gingerly laying Astrielle on the padded surface, covering her with a red scarf.

The door to the bedroom creaked open and Astrielle stirred, her eyes slowly opening. It took her a moment to remember where she was and when she did she was pleased to see Miran. "Where am I?" she asked.

"Good morning, little friend," smiled Miran.

Astrielle smiled back. "Good morning, big rescuer!"

"Welcome to my home. I'm glad to see you're okay. I was worried about you."

Astrielle, grimacing in pain, tried to stretch her wings. Craning her neck, she saw her wing was bent. "Ooooh, my poor, poor wing," she lamented.

Miran set the tray on a table. "Let me take a look at it."

The wing was not only bent, it was also crumpled. Miran attempted to straighten it, but Astrielle winced at her touch. "Be gentle, now."

"You *are* delicate, aren't you?"

"Yes, I'm fragile as a flower, a new budding spring one…and bright pink, too." She giggled.

"You're lucky you survived, you know."

"I thought I was dinner for sure."

"Speaking of eating, are you hungry?"

"I'm famished! Fighting off oraks builds up an appetite."

Miran set a small plate of cooked grains in front of Astrielle, who ate ravenously. "It wasn't luck," she said. "It was you, young warrior. You saved me. I owe you my life."

"Well, then. I'll think of something you can do for me."

"Anything at all!" Astrielle exclaimed.

"What's your name?" Miran asked.

"Astrielle."

"Very pretty."

"Thank you," Astrielle said, taking another bite.

"What were you doing out so late all by yourself?"

"I was flying home from the courtyard, and I was so very tired from working, I must have fallen asleep and…oh no!" Her fork stopped in mid-air.

"What is it?" asked Miran.

"I'm supposed to be there now, helping them get ready for the Sultana's visit." She paused, a sadness overtaking her. "They say this is going to be her last trip to the Fairy Forest."

Miran found this sentiment heartwarming. The fairies were always so thoughtful. "So I've heard."

"Even a young warrior like you knows…" She looked at Miran expectantly.

"Go on."

"Well, the Sultana is very ill and will be stepping down from the throne soon." She looked sad again. "Isn't that sad?"

It was sad, yes. In more ways than the fairy knew. But Miran chose not to trouble Astrielle with her problems. "Yes, it is," she said.

Miran was going to ask Astrielle more about herself but was interrupted by the sound of a knock at the front door. They had arrived.

Miran's mother opened the front door of the cottage. There stood two High Council members. The older one, Dosha, had jet black hair, streaked with white and a face that radiated joy. The other, Bajo, was younger and decidedly more stern, her strawberry blond hair pulled back into a tight bun, making her sour face even more tart.

Adean led them into the sitting room and asked them to sit down.

Dosha, smiling broadly, spoke first, gesturing with her hands. "Adean, we are very excited. The royal residence has been working around the clock preparing the castle for Miran's arrival. She will come to us in just a few days to live at the palace in seclusion. After twenty-eight days of preparation, she will be crowned Sultana! On the new moons!" Dosha glowed in anticipation of this great day.

Adean, overflowing with pride, smiled in return. "We are very pleased," she said.

Bajo remained serious, almost solemn. "It will be the end of an era," she said, her voice cracking. Her eyes began to well up. She tried to keep the tears in, wiping them away with the sleeve of her cloak, but there was no stopping the flood. Dosha put an arm around her friend and this caused Bajo to cry harder and more loudly.

"If there's any chance that Sultana Henrit can continue, Miran can wait—" Adean said.

Freya sat at a table in the corner, practicing a weaving exercise. Long strands of yellow, green and blue flowed from a small wooden frame. "I don't want to wait," she blurted out. "I want to live in the castle now."

Adean gave Freya a look.

"And so you shall," said Dosha happily. "Sultana Henrit has been well loved, and we will all miss her. But she is fading quickly. She won't live more than a couple of seasons. She knows as well as anyone that we must prepare for Miran's arrival."

This comment propelled Bajo into a fresh wave of sobbing.

Astrielle, who had been listening intently, understood everything in an instant. She looked at Miran, her eyes widening. "You! You're going to be the next Sultana!"

Miran grinned and held out her hand. "Come with me."

With effort, Astrielle climbed into the palm of Miran's hand and down the hallway they went. Miran stopped, peeking from behind the corner, and saw her mother with Dosha and Bajo.

Dosha continued. "Miran's chosen mate is Grideon. He has been approved by the High Council and has accepted the role of Sultan. He will undergo his own preparations before they marry. Following the ceremony, Grideon will come and go as duty dictates."

Bajo, having finished with crying for the moment, dabbed her eyes and addressed Adean. "There is a rumor that Miran has reservations about becoming Sultana."

Adean wasn't surprised. They had probably heard this rumor from the other girls. Miran's ambivalence wasn't a secret. However, if Miran didn't become Sultana, Anay would take her place and that would mean disaster. She must do whatever was needed to keep that from happening; but more than that, she believed in her daughter's ability to fulfill her role as Sultana.

She waved her hand dismissively. "Of course she has fears about it, as any young warrior would, but she will adjust to her new responsibilities. There's no doubt about that."

"We must return to the castle," said Bajo.

"Yes. Thank you, Adean," added Dosha.

Freya pulled strands one at a time, aligning them in a crisscross pattern. "Mama, this is going to be my headpiece for the coronation ceremony."

"Lovely, Freya," said Adean.

As Adean saw Dosha and Bajo out, Freya's mind drifted. *And afterwards, we'll all live in the castle together. Yes, that will be fun.* She looked up to see her big sister with an unfamiliar fairy sitting in her hand.

"Beautiful work, little sister," said Miran.

"Who is that?"

Adean came back and said to Miran, "I thought I heard voices coming from your room."

Greet and Vita paused their cleaning.

"Aren't you Astrielle?" asked Vita.

Astrielle nodded. "Vita, is that you?"

"Yes! We grew up together, Greet."

"Well!" Greet exclaimed.

"Her wing is injured, Mother," Miran said.

Astrielle beamed. "Your daughter saved me from a hungry orak at the last minute. She was *so* brave."

"You must have been terrified," Adean said, examining the wing. "You'll be fine. After a visit to Heggor, it'll be like new. I just shudder to think what would've happened if Miran hadn't come along, you poor thing."

"She'd be dead and eaten," Freya said.

"Freya!" scolded her mother.

Miran and Astrielle burst into laughter.

Healing Arts

Heggor the Healer lived in a stone cottage in the heart of the forest with her daughter Thaya. A large boned woman with scraggly grey hair and sparkling blue eyes, Heggor always gave the impression she had just recently been physically exerting herself, which was usually true.

Thaya was almost a perfect replica of her mother, except for her ash blond hair and the multitude of freckles she had inherited from her father. Although still an apprentice, she had mastered the basics of how to use roots, leaves and flowers indigenous to the island, along with magik, to cure any ailment.

The mother-daughter pair lived in an esoteric world of potions, tinctures, poultices and spells. Their days were dominated by collecting materials from the forest, harvesting leaves and flowers that would create the most potent medicines that made up a vast pharmacopeia.

They had perfected the art of healing by tapping into the highest energy fields that were hidden away in nature, learning to sense subtle vibrations and discovering the right combinations of elements which brought on the desired reaction. When there was imbalance in the body, either inflicted from the outside or originating internally, it meant the energy flow was blocked or imbalanced. Their job was to clear the blockage and allow the energy—the life force—to flow freely again.

There were thousands of cures they could perform on the spot, and many curatives that could be made ready in a matter of minutes. Other remedies required longer to mature and become potent. These had to be made ready ahead of time; today they were preparing one of those.

Thaya held a basket full of blue ornh fruit blossoms, each the size of a fist. She observed the mixture simmering inside the enormous black pot as it gathered heat from the fire below. Two hundred flowers had to be boiled for five hours in the cream of the bark of the crimson bantan tree.

She tipped the basket and the blossoms tumbled into the steaming liquid, turning it a deep indigo color. As the temperature increased, the brew bubbled and foamed, the steam rising up and escaping through an opening in the roof.

Heggor came over to check the consistency. Satisfied with what she saw, she told Thaya to pour the last basket of blooms into the pot. Thaya lowered a long wooden spoon into the concoction, melding the substances together. Blue steam lifted off the surface, swirling up through the hole and dissipating into corners of the room.

Once the liquid evaporated, they scooped out what was left—a fine indigo paste—and spooned it into large shallow bowls. The paste would be dried for three days, then ground into a soft powder and stored in jars, then labeled and stacked on shelves.

Astrielle, aside from the occasional twinge in her wing, had ridden comfortably in Miran's pocket. She noticed the blue smoke before she saw the cottage it came from. A bitter taste hung in the air, metallic and gritty. "What is that terrible stink?" She held her nose in distaste.

Miran crinkled her nose as well. "There's always a myriad of strange odors here. You'll get used to it."

"I don't think so!"

Miran came down from Cavalo's back and knocked at the cottage door.

Thaya's voice rang out from inside, "Coming!"

In a few moments, a blue eye appeared in the peephole. "Miran!" she exclaimed, opening the door, her plump figure filling the threshold.

"Hello, Thaya!" Miran replied.

Thaya's rosy face, dotted with all those freckles, was full of smiles and good cheer. Wiping the sweat from her brow, she said, "Lovely to see you. Who's your friend?"

"This is Astrielle."

"Please come in." She led them into the waiting area. "Welcome, Astrielle."

Thaya turned to the back of the cottage. "Mother! Miran's here!"

"Be there shortly!" Heggor yelled back.

"Is something ailing you, dear?" Thaya asked.

"Nothing's wrong with me," Miran answered. "It's Astrielle—"

Heggor emerged from behind the curtain. Roughened red cheeks framed her round face and her weathered hands, calloused and strong, danced as she spoke. "My dear Miran! You have grown so! Now what is the trouble?"

Thaya, in her eagerness, didn't wait for Miran to respond. "Oh, Mother! Come see. It's an injured fairy!"

Heggor didn't need to ask what was wrong, of course. She had developed a sixth sense, could detect the source of discord without being told. "You, my fairy friend, have a broken wing don't you now?" She looked at Miran. "And, you, my dear, have a bite on your hand."

Miran opened her mouth in disbelief. "You always know."

"Come along, then." Heggor held out her hand to Astrielle, who climbed on. Miran and Thaya followed Heggor into the healing room. Baskets were scattered about, each laden with a different species of twig, bark or a motley assortment of the parts of dead animals.

Against the wall, tall shelves were packed with jars filled with powders, liquids, pastes and serums.

Heggor placed Astrielle onto a soft pillow.

"Yes," mused Heggor, examining the wing. "It's just as I suspected." She thought for a moment, her forefinger at her chin. Then she clapped her hands. "The green solace poultice, Thaya."

"I know, Mother," said Thaya, already reaching for the bottle.

"All right, child. If you know so much, you can heal this little fairy's wing very nicely on your own." Heggor winked at them and left the room.

Suddenly Thaya wasn't so confident. It was one thing to know the appropriate poultice, and quite another to apply it correctly. She was able to provoke the magikal healing energy sometimes, but other times she failed. She paused, wishing her mother hadn't put her on the spot like this. She smiled awkwardly. "I will have your wing healed in a jiffy," she said, her tone hollow.

Astrielle glanced apprehensively at Miran.

"I know you will," said Miran, mustering as much certainty as she could.

Thaya unscrewed the cork and pulled a small cloth from a drawer. She tipped the bottle, saturating the center of the fabric with the poultice. Then, very delicately, she applied the salve to Astrielle's wing. "Might sting a bit…"

Astrielle winced. Thaya put the cloth down and began the hardest part, the magik invocation. That, combined with the power of the medicine, was the secret to every healing; the vibration of sound merging with the vibration of matter. Each, on its own, was weak and inconsistent, but together they harnessed the power of infinite intelligence.

Thaya was on her way to becoming a Supreme Healer and she felt a surge of pride every time she was successful. One day she would replace Heggor and in turn would teach her own daughter, when she had one, the art of healing. This tradition would go on for generations, the passing down of knowledge and wisdom.

She pulled a wand from her cloak, raised it to the ceiling and concentrated on the tip of it. Closing her throat slightly, she inhaled through her nose, forcing the air through, producing a wheezing sound. The end of the wand glowed a light shade of citrine. She exhaled through her mouth, with the same sound, but louder. The glow intensified and grew to cover the length of the wand.

Slowly, she moved the wand in line with Astrielle's wing as she chanted the spell that went with the poultice. She used the ancient Zarada tongue, no longer spoken, but still intoned for ceremonies and spells.

She repeated over and over, "Prahada, Gredama, Hradaman." The wand shook and buzzed. She held on tightly and continued, "Prahada, Gredama, Hradaman."

The wand, attracted to the place where the poultice had been applied, fluttered, projecting a shaft of light to Astrielle's injured wing. The crumpled wing absorbed the glow, straightening and smoothing out under the influence of the healing magik. Astrielle's pained expression turned to wonder, then relief.

Thaya, too, was relieved. She broke into a laugh, her whole body chuckling along with her. "Well, try it out!"

The little fairy fluttered her wings and her face lit up. "It's all better!" she chirped with joy.

Thaya, a bit surprised herself, quickly remembered to complete the procedure while the light was still aglow. She chanted again. "Trehama, Srukeeda, Gredama."

The light in the wand flickered and died. Thaya slid it back into its sheath, happy with her handiwork. "Yes, well, that's how it works, when it works!"

Miran said, "I knew you could do it."

Astrielle flapped her wings and flew about the room, delighted to have her freedom back. "Thank you, Thaya. It feels like new now. Perfect."

Even though she had been in good hands, Astrielle was glad to be mobile again. Without wings, fairies were vulnerable and helpless, subject to predators that could swallow them down in one bite. They had to be able to fly in an instant up to the treetops where it was safe. If Astrielle couldn't fly, she was as good as dead.

Astrielle remembered Miran's hand. "Your turn," she said.

"It's nothing," said Miran, hiding her hand. "I hardly feel it."

Thaya ignored Miran's comment. Her confidence up, she pulled a different bottle off the shelf. With a different incantation and another glow of the wand, Miran's skin was healed over.

"Now it's nothing," teased Thaya.

Miran hadn't wanted to admit it, but her hand *had* been hurting. Now that the pain was gone, she was grateful. "Thank you," she said.

Thaya called out, "I'm finished, Mother!"

Heggor came back to inspect her daughter's work. She nodded in approval. "Excellent, Thaya. Well done!"

Thaya stood a bit taller and a smile as big as her heart opened wide across her rosy, freckled face.

Selexi's True Colors

Twice every moon cycle, the young warriors played a game called discs. Metal discs were tossed back and forth, caught by mitts with magnets inside them which attracted the discs. The object of the game was to score goals at either end of the field.

Selex was in the royal tier. She lounged in a soft, luxurious chair, waiting for the game to begin. As daughter of the Sultana, she had lived in the castle all her life, taking advantage of all the grandeur and conveniences while all the time feeling envious of the power her mother possessed.

When she had become pregnant with Anay, and the predicted time of birth pointed to her child becoming the next Sultana, she thought she held a golden ace in her womb. She could not now accept the idea that when Miran became Sultana, she would have to leave the castle and live in a common cottage.

Gaining control over the island and being the one they all obeyed; *that* was a vision so delicious she couldn't help losing herself in the dark joy of it. But nothing had gone the way she had planned. Her lips snaked into a sneer as she indulged her bitter malice. *It has all been ruined by that little runt. I must stop her. I will not stand by while she assumes the throne. I will find a way.*

Selexi's dying mother reclined a few feet away. The frail Sultana had been advised by Heggor to stay in today, but she hated to miss a game and so was brought out at her own insistence. She seemed relatively alert, but Selexi knew it was only a matter of time before she succumbed to the disease. *Soon*, Selexi mused, *that old crone will be dead.*

Adean, hoping to get by the royal tier unnoticed, entered the stadium, Freya by her side. She kept her gaze forward. Selexi was always impossible to deal with.

"Adean," Selexi called out.

Adean braced herself. She looked at Selexi suspiciously. "Greetings," she replied briskly.

She was going to continue walking but was caught off guard by the sight of the Sultana. The last time she had seen her, the elderly woman had been up and around, weak perhaps but able to walk fairly well with the help of her cane. Now she seemed half her size, her face a pallid yellow color. Adean, shocked at what she saw, moved closer to the railing. "Sultana, it's so good to see you. How are you feeling?"

"Old," the Sultana answered. "But my mind is sharper than ever. How is my young successor?"

Selexi mocked the question. "Yes, how is she?" she echoed, a hiss woven in her words.

"Growing up, and too quickly, I'm afraid," replied Adean. "But she's a good girl, and we're very pleased she'll be moving to the castle soon."

The Sultana thought of her own granddaughter. *Was she a good girl? No, she wasn't. Was she pleased with her? Not at all. Anay had been good at one time, long ago, but her mother had tainted her. Now she was spoiled.*

"Our Anay is also no longer a child," the Sultana said. "Those girls are the future of this island now."

Selexi couldn't resist chiming in. "How can you say Anay is the future of this island? Let's not pretend, Mother. Miran is the future. She's the one you're talking about."

"Selexi, please," said the Sultana. "Anay is a citizen of this island and her role is just as important as anyone else's. And if she wants to, she can hold an important position in the High Council, or even at the Academy. She has the makings of a great Zaradian if she chooses to be."

Selexi sniffed. "It's not the position she was meant for."

"Perhaps there's a reason for that," countered the Sultana.

"As far as I'm concerned, all the young warriors of Zarada are part of our future," Adean said.

"Yes," agreed the Sultana. "They are."

Selexi opened her mouth again to throw more unpleasantness into the conversation, but the gong sounded, signaling the start of play.

Freya laughed at Selexi's open mouth, the sound of the gong seeming to ring directly out of it. Adean, relieved that the confrontation was over, nodded to the Sultana, met Selexi's cool gaze for a moment, then turned and led Freya up to their seats.

Rivals

Miran slid a silver helmet over her head as she ran onto the playing field with her teammates. Because of the water shortage and the intense heat, the High Council considered cancelling the game, but the girls begged to allow the game to proceed. The Council acquiesced, allowing them half the normal length of time to prevent dehydration.

Miran and her team wore burnt-orange sport halters and tight black shorts that ended mid-thigh. The opposing team, headed by Anay, wore mossy-green tanks with the same shorts in blue, their names visible on the backs of their helmets. They wore black shoes and high socks with shin guards.

Every player wore a mitt on one hand, the pocket of each mitt lined with a magnetic attraction that pulled the disc into it. With enough force, the disc could be whipped from the mitt, or simply pried away with the other hand to be thrown to another team player. Once a player had the disc, they could sprint with it or pass it to other players before they were tackled. If the disc touched the ground, the team who dropped it had to give it to the other side. There were penalties and three of them resulted in the loss of five points. As soon as a goal was made, ten points were earned.

The object of the game was for each team to work together to get as many discs as possible into their respective nets at each end of the field. Every net also had a magnetic field inside it. Once the discs entered the field, they floated in a state of suspension and the referee would produce another disc to continue the play.

The players began warming up, tossing discs back and forth, running to retrieve stray discs. The large playing field, normally lush and green, was dusty and dry from the drought. Puffs of dirt swirled around their feet as the players jockeyed for position.

The gong sounded. The referee blew the whistle and the practice discs were collected. The players, five to a team, took their places on the center line. The referee stood in the middle, a team on either side, keeping the disc safely tucked in the crook of her elbows. She opened her arms, letting the disc roll down into her cupped hands. She grasped it between her thumbs and forefingers and slowly raised it above her head, holding it high for a dramatic pause.

The crowd cheered in anticipation as the sterling disc glinted in the harsh rays of the suns. The referee bent her elbows and knees, bringing the disc almost to the ground and in a sweep threw it as hard as she could straight up into the air, sending it far out of sight. The rule was that during the throw, all the players had to keep their feet in place. Teammates leaned toward each other, holding their mitts up in clusters, trying to attract the disc with collective force.

When the disc came whooshing down with a whine it landed *pop* into Thiggy's mitt, one of Anay's teammates. She ran toward the goal along with everyone else. Seeing an opening to pass, she aimed and tossed it over the heads of the other players.

Satrah, who was on Miran's team, leaped for it. She intercepted it but just as it fell into Satrah's mitt, Anay lunged and grabbed Satrah by the calves. Satrah fell into the dust, dropping the disc. Anay's violation caused the whistle to sound. The referee cried out, "Off!!"

Anay was benched. There were other methods of getting the disc away from an opponent. Grabbing ankles was not allowed.

After a few uneventful rounds, Anay was allowed back in. She caught the disc and ran swiftly, tossing it to another teammate as the other team was crowding in on her. Miran reached out with her mitt and the disc was suspended in midair, caught between the attractions of her mitt and the mitt of another girl who was trying to catch it. It was a standoff. Miran's team gathered around her and Anay's team gathered around and the two teams used their magnetic strength in an attempt to pull the disc into their possession.

Anay's eyes bore into Miran with rage and determination, the wind of unfulfilled desire fanning the fire within her until it became a consuming blaze of hatred. Unable to hold back any longer, she sprung forward, grabbing Miran by the throat. The referee rushed over to restrain her but got one of Anay's boots in the face and dropped to the ground, unconscious.

The crowd bounded to their feet, shocked by the violence, unheard of during a game. The Sultana was shocked and embarrassed. This was *her grandchild* making an unnecessary scene. She signaled for help. Selexi remained comfortably seated in her front row royal chair, thoroughly enjoying her daughter's display of dominance.

Adean was relieved to see that the Sultana was taking care of the matter.

With no one to stop her, Anay pushed Miran down into the dirt, straddling her, pinning her arms to the ground. Miran struggled but was no match for Anay. At last, the guards arrived. They pulled Anay away from Miran and took her off the playing field. The game was declared over, forfeited by Anay's team.

Miran got to her feet. Satrah asked if she was all right. She told her she was but she couldn't have felt more wrong.

Selexi's Laboratory

Night descended. The moons peered down like askew yellow eyes set in a sunken skull. If their gaze could penetrate deeper than sky and land, going beneath the island, their light would have found Selexi.

She spent most of her time in her secret laboratory, conducting perverse experiments that combined magik and malice. No more than a dank cavity, this murky cave, this den of evil doing, was the only source of pleasure she had, albeit twisted and cruel.

A long table dominated the room, beakers, flasks and tubes meandering in a serpentine maze across it. A stack of cages perched haphazardly against the far wall and inside the cages lurked an assortment of hideous creatures—her collection of mutants.

These oddities, the result of trial and error, spent most of their time sleeping. They might have been better off put out of their misery, but Selexi's ego prevented her from destroying them. They were her most prized accomplishments, a constant reminder of her genius. She often neglected to feed them on time, and they were overdue for a feeding now. They scratched, screeched, and whined, until she yielded.

"Pesky things!" she scolded. Pulling out a canvas bag, she carried it to the corner and scooped coarse meal into their trays. "I should have put you all out of your pitiful existence long ago," she growled. "The amount you cost me in gruel!" They cowered at her words as their snouts delved into the food. "Nothing but a nuisance, the lot of you. Useless! And, ugly besides!"

They were indeed grotesque things, living a pitiable existence, but they had never known any other life. The only kindness they had ever received was from Anay, who brought them treats and talked to them nicely. They licked the dry meal from the bottoms of their cages, snorting noisily, then lay down again to lose themselves to slumber.

Against another wall, tall towers of books rose precariously, like a city full of decaying buildings. Piled high from floor to ceiling, the subjects of the books ranged from chemistry to alchemy, biology to magik.

Since her youth, Selexi had been scrupulous in her acquisition of knowledge and relentless in her pursuit of the mastery of these subjects. Not only had she read them all, she also understood them totally; how the different areas of study worked individually, but more importantly, the great power they possessed when they were combined correctly.

She surveyed the kaleidoscope of substances on her worktable: a myriad of textures and colors in the forms of viscous liquids, sparkling crystals, luminous powders and churning elixirs. Pungent aromas leaked from vessels large and small. One concoction, bright green, bubbled, threatened to overflow. Another sprouted a deep yellow crystalline formation that grew ever so slowly but was worth the wait—it was a replica of an expensive gem used for women's jewelry.

But these experiments were simple alchemy. She was onto something much bigger now, a new mutant she had worked on in complete secrecy. She hadn't even told Anay about it.

A diminutive creature requiring no food or water, obeying without question and killing on demand, she called this mutant a keru. It was designed to be free of emotions and personal attachments, taking orders only from Selexi. Her plan was to mass produce them and create an army of them. With this army she would have the capability to take over the island.

If she had put her skills to a higher purpose, Selexi might have been revered for her contributions toward the betterment of life on Zarada. Her sheer brainpower was boundless. But she was not interested in a higher purpose. Quite the opposite. She was as ruthless as she was brilliant and her keen intelligence coupled with a power-hungry obsession gave her everything she needed to fabricate her devious plan unchecked.

She was so very close to reaching her goal now, but time was running thin. She had to move quickly or lose her chance forever.

The Last Visit

Sultana Henrit was helped into the golden carriage where she rested her frail body in the soft red velvet seat. A burgundy gown fit loosely on her slender frame and small golden slippers adorned her dainty feet. A silver crown studded with red and yellow gems perched around her fountain of white hair.

This will be my last ride through this magnificent forest, she thought sadly. *The last time I see my dear fairies.*

Raina climbed in after her, arranging cushions. The driver gave a shout to the team and the four white camions galloped over the dusty path.

A blur of trees raced past and they gained speed until there was a powerful thrust upward and the carriage was lifted into the sky by the camions. The Sultana looked out the window, down at her treasured island growing smaller beneath her. She was pained by how brown it had become, regretting the suffering of the animals and plants. Her people were suffering, too. They were on their last reserves of water and food.

There was only one solution—to call the rain. They needed the red larimar stones that came from Saron. Yet no one worthy of the task had come forth to offer to retrieve them. They had depended upon the reserves to nourish them while they figured out who to send to Saron, but mold had crept in and spread, tainting all they had. Now they were in danger of losing everything, even their lives.

They were approaching the fairy forest. The thought of seeing her dear fairies distracted her out of her worries. The fairies suddenly appeared around the carriage, flitting here, then there, up and around, circling and veering, flashes of sunlight dancing rainbows on their luminescent wings. Astrielle was among them, chirping happily at the arrival of her beloved Sultana.

The Sultana's heart burst with delight to hear the twinkling of lively music and the glittering of dazzling lights. The carriage dropped down as they made their descent. The camion's hooves met the path and they barreled down the road, coming to a halt at the fairy courtyard.

When she emerged, fairy dust fell down upon her from high in the treetops as fairies flew around, giggling with delight. She smiled and waved at them and Raina handed her the cane to help her gain her footing. They were led to their seats while royal harmonies, played by the little orchestra, filled the air with familiar tunes.

The Fairy King and Queen landed on the stage and all the fairies cheered. "We welcome you, our beloved Sultana!" exclaimed the King.

"Let the show begin!" declared the Queen.

Fairies by the thousands rained down from the sky and flew in a dancing pattern that went with the music. After that, the curtain parted to reveal a stage. A musical was performed that retold the story of the Zaradians and their friendship with the fairies. Jugglers and magicians entertained next, with a hypnotic display of clever tricks and dizzying stunts.

When the show was over, the Sultana rose. Applause erupted, then quieted as the Sultana raised her hand. There was important business to discuss—the real reason for her visit.

The look on her face let them know she was delighted by their efforts, but they were worried when they saw how she strained to remain standing, how she leaned heavily on her cane. She was indeed ailing, but the regal poise she had exhibited throughout her rule was still fully present and as commanding as ever. "Great and loyal fairies," she began. "I am here with joy and sadness in my heart. You have been cherished friends and allies my whole life long."

The fairies buzzed their wings and tittered in agreement.

"We have survived many challenges together, haven't we? Our bond has never wavered. But, my cherished ones, the time has come for me to pass the torch to a new leader. The next Sultana will be Miran, daughter of Adean, granddaughter of Galanee."

The crowd murmured their mixed emotions.

"Do not be sad, my friends. Be joyous! Celebrate the time we've had and extend your loyal friendship to my successor, who will continue..." The Sultana coughed. "...who will continue where I left...?"

The Fairy Queen looked on helplessly, pained by the sight.

The Sultana bent forward slightly and coughed again, her voice cracking as she recovered her composure. "...where I left off. I will take memories of you to the next plane of existence. Peace be with you all!"

The fairies cheered as loudly as fairies can, more a mixture of flapping, giggling and sighing. The Sultana's body hunched over, but her eyes shone brightly as she gazed upon the multitude of sweet beings that were so dear to her heart. She smiled warmly as she drank in the sight of her friends one last time.

The music began again and the audience took their cue, dispersing in an instant, leaving the Sultana alone with the King and Queen. With Raina's help, the Sultana sat back down and caught her breath. "That was a lovely performance," she gushed. "Don't you think so Raina?"

"Absolutely brilliant," Raina agreed.

The Fairy Queen smiled adoringly at the Sultana. "We are so glad you enjoyed it. We wanted to make it extra special for you."

The King, never one for small talk, cleared his throat. "We were uncertain that you'd come."

"Today, I feel that I could go on for some time. Tomorrow may be different. But enough about that! What news do you have of the grain shoots? Any sign of growth after the experimental irrigation?"

The Fairy Queen's demeanor turned grim. She glanced worriedly at the King before addressing the Sultana. "Nothing yet. There wasn't enough of the desalinated water to make a difference. If we don't have rain soon, there will be no crops."

The Sultana frowned. "The sea vegetables have been over harvested as it is."

The Queen wrung her tiny hands together. "Something has to be done."

"Without the red larimar stones, we face certain famine," added the King.

The Sultana nodded. "We lost Galanee, our last great stone hunter, to the red larimar fields and the daemons. No one has stepped forward to take her place."

"Someone has got to make the trip," said the King. "Immediately."

The Queen nodded in agreement. "Yes they must."

The Sultana knew they were right. "It is a treacherous journey, with perilous risks, but I will find someone. They must be brave enough and strong enough. And willing enough. With all our strong warriors, there will be one with the courage."

There was nothing more to discuss. They said their goodbyes with tears that fell from the knowledge that it would be the last time they would see each other.

Once inside the carriage, the Sultana collapsed back against the cushions and closed her tired eyes, barely hearing the driver command the camions into flight before she succumbed to sleep.

A Chance for Anay

Selexi's house fairies Eyla and Myla were especially mischievous and rebellious. This was due largely to Selexi's poor treatment of them. She addressed them harshly, showing none of the warmth that fairies thrive on and making it clear that in her eyes they were no more than pesky necessities. She had gone through many fairies over the years because none of them could tolerate her rudeness for very long.

Eyla and Myla were always getting into trouble and this evening was no exception. They had made a game of turning the makeup box into a playground. Anay, sitting in front of the vanity mirror, hardly noticed them as they plunged brushes into the face powder and spun in circles, peals of laughter bursting from their delicate mouths. They threw handfuls of powder at each other, covering themselves and the tabletop, scattering it every which way.

When Selexi came in the room, they immediately stopped their antics and stifled their giggles. Seeing the mess, she glared at them and slammed the makeup box shut, *clack!*—almost pinching Myla's hand in the process. Stomping her foot and waving her arms, she reproached, "Eyla, Myla. Out! Shoo!"

The fairies cowered, slinking away, making apologetic faces as they flew off. But as soon as they were out the door, they mocked Selexi. "Out! Shoo!" they mimicked, producing glissandos of laughter and somersaults in midair.

Ignoring the sounds of the fairies, Selexi stood behind Anay, gauging her daughter's mood. She picked up a brush and began passing it through Anay's long golden hair.

Anay opened an eye shadow box, chose a brush and applied a layer of cool grey to her eyelids. She followed that with a shade of hazel, then shimmering gold above, finishing with sparkling white. Her exquisite green eyes shone back at her.

"You know you are the most beautiful young warrior on this island," Selexi said. "As well as the strongest."

Anay's eyes flashed up at her mother suspiciously. "Don't start, Mother."

Ignoring Anay's warning, Selexi continued. "I had the pleasure of being the Sultana's daughter all my life. I had the glamour, but none of the power. My mother always lectured me. She said that instead of appreciating my high station of privilege, I resented that I would not have the chance to be Sultana myself. Well, of course that was true. How could it not be? I, with all my brilliance, was supposed to be satisfied with less than what I was capable of?"

Anay wished her mother would go away.

But Selexi went on. "I decided I would have the next best thing. That's why I timed your conception perfectly. What triumph I felt when I learned I was to give birth to the next Sultana! I knew that it was through you that I would rule this island. But a cruel twist of events interfered with my plan." Selexi's face darkened. "I remember the moment when the announcement came that Miran had been born early."

Something grabbed Anay's attention. "You planned my conception? You never told me that."

"Well, how else was I supposed to ensure that I stay in the castle?"

Anay wanted more than anything to be Sultana. But there was a part of her that wanted to have it fairly. The idea of taking it without earning it violated her need to know it was her rightful place. She shook her head in disbelief. "You're even more conniving than I thought."

It was always the same theme with her mother— always the same conversation. She didn't like the situation either, but sometimes she wished that her mother would let it go. She put on a face of toughness with Miran, and wanted to be Sultana more than anything, but if there was no chance she could be, then deep down she wanted the feud to end. What good did it do to pour salt on the wound?

It did feel good to have her hair brushed like that. And she hadn't finished putting on her makeup. She would just have to steer her mother into another direction.

"So, your 'plan' didn't work and so there's nothing more to discuss. Let's talk about the Academy. They've offered me a position there after I graduate. I'm thinking of taking it."

"Are you?" Selexi had an agenda but didn't want to risk triggering Anay's temper and sudden departure. She feigned compliance with silence and continued running the brush over her daughter's tresses, with the intention of lulling her into a calm, receptive state. Then she started up again.

"Look at that golden blond hair, those shimmering eyes…" She hesitated for a moment, the old anger brimming over the edges of her mind. She couldn't stop herself from showing disdain. "The eyes of a Sultana…ugh. If it hadn't been for Miran's early birth…you would be preparing now and I would be—"

"Will you stop?!" Anay's head whipped around. "I've heard it enough times already. Just finish brushing so I can leave." She picked up another makeup applicator and a clay pot. Dipping the brush into the pot, she lightly blushed her cheeks with the shimmering pink powder.

Selexi bristled. "I will never give up on you and your destiny."

"I don't like it any more than you do, Mother, but what's done is done. Miran is going to be our next Sultana. There's nothing we can do. I don't want to hear any more about it. Not ever again."

Selexi began pinning her daughter's hair into a complex pattern of braids. "Yes, that is the law, my pet. *The first girl born after the rise of the second moon shall rule the land.*"

"Yes, yes. I know."

Selexi paused, wanting her words to have their full impact. "But did you know that there is another law that will allow you to become Sultana and force Miran out of the circle of power forever?" Selexi waited and watched for the desired response.

Anay hesitated. She didn't want to build up her hopes, but she *was* curious.

Selexi grinned. *Good, I have her attention.*

Anay took in her mother's image in the mirror, trying to understand. "What are you talking about? What law?"

Selexi didn't say a word, but a smirk deepened across her lips.

Anay spun around, her eyes raptly fixed on Selexi's. "Tell me. Now."

Selexi savored the moment, taking her time. She laid the hairbrush on the vanity table and placed her hands firmly on her daughter's shoulders. "I've been waiting for the right moment to tell you. The time has finally come for you to learn the truth." She turned and walked away. "Come with me, child."

It was easier to pretend she didn't care. She had tried to suppress the desire to be Sultana all her life and was finally ready to accept that it would never come to be. Did she dare imagine it could miraculously be fulfilled by some obscure law? Or was her mother just devising another scheme that would never materialize?

It was too tempting to rule out the possibility. *I'll hear her out, then decide.* She followed her mother down the hallway and into the library.

Selexi climbed the rolling ladder that straddled one of the enormous bookshelves and pulled out a large tree-leather bound volume. It was so heavy, Selexi almost lost her balance as it tumbled into her arms. Anay helped her carry the book to a podium that rested on top of a large carved wooden table facing the bay window.

She read the title on the cover, *"The Laws of Zarada."* She looked at Selexi. "We have studied sections of this at The Academy."

"Not the part I'm about to show you." Selexi flipped through the book, located the spot she was looking for and ran her finger along the page. "Here it is." She tapped the paragraph with her forefinger. "Right here. Read it out loud."

Anay leaned over and read the words. *"Regarding claims to the title of Sultana: If there is another girl born in the same moon cycle as the First Born who wishes to prove her superiority, she may initiate a challenge for the title of Sultana. They must go on a quest of the Sultana's choice. If the challenger proves to be more worthy, she may claim the throne.*"

"You see?" Selexi said encouragingly. "The throne is yours for the taking. And take it you will."

"Why didn't you tell me about this before?"

"A challenge is an enormous undertaking with many risks. I thought Miran would give up the throne out of weakness by now and save us the trouble of declaring a challenge. She may still do just that, especially when she finds out she has to compete against you. Even if she does accept, she is no match for you. So, you see—the throne is yours for the taking. All yours."

Smugness played on Anay's face. She walked to the window and her distorted reflection looked back at her from the dark glass. Her eyes flashed with ferocity and the words fell from her lips in a low whisper, "I can be Sultana."

Selexi came up behind her, the reflection of her face eerily misshapen by imperfections in the window. "You *will* be Sultana."

83

The Sultana's Revelation

The bondo licked the last traces of dew from a brittle blade of foliage. Weakened by the effort, he crawled to a shady spot behind a bush, closed his eyes and sank his emaciated body into the parched moss to sleep the day away.

Anay awoke early. Shaking off the covers, she got out of bed and pulled a robe over her sleeping gown then peeked into Selexi's room, making sure her mother was sleeping

She quietly snuck out of their quarters and walked briskly through the wide castle hallways, passing cooks, housemaids and guards. They took no notice of her. When she arrived at the door of her grandmother's wing, she knocked.

The Sultana found the strength that morning to go to her study. She hadn't sat at her desk in weeks but had felt an unexpected surge of energy and decided to use it to catch up on correspondence. There were letters piling up on her desk and she replied to them. Her pen now hovered over the bottom of the letter she had completed.

As she put down her signature, she wondered if it was the last occasion she would have to sign her name.

She put one to the side and moved on to the next one. It was addressed to the leader of Yad. Halfway through it, she heard voices outside the door. She had an idea who her early morning visitor was. A minute later, her suspicion was confirmed; Anay, her only grandchild, stood in the doorway, impetuous and impatient as usual.

"It's Anay," announced Raina.

"You may come in," Henrit said, and then brought her attention back to the letter.

Anay ventured closer. She had been so anxious to come, but now that she was here she was at a loss for words. Maybe it had been a mistake. She didn't know where to begin.

"What brings you here, my dear?" the Sultana asked, signing the letter and placing it on top of the pile.

"Well," Anay started. "I came to see how you're feeling."

The Sultana peered more closely at her granddaughter. "What are you cooking up, you and that mother of yours? She hasn't allowed you to visit me in many moons." Her eyes narrowed further. "She must want something."

"She doesn't even know I'm here."

"I see."

"It's not my choice, you know. I would come more often if I could but she wouldn't like it. You won't tell her will you?"

"I won't say a word," the Sultana assured her. "Enough about her. Let's talk about you. I hear you're a great warrior in the making. How are your studies coming along?"

"I'm the strongest young warrior by far," Anay boasted.

"Physical strength is only one aspect. Not the most important, as you'll find out someday."

"You're wrong. It's the only thing that matters in the end."

The Sultana was too tired to argue. "What's on your mind, child?" she asked. "You never pay a visit without an ulterior motive. What is it this time?"

"Don't you want me to be the next Sultana?"

The Sultana sighed. "I've told you many times before—I don't have an opinion about it. I didn't choose to be Sultana, and neither can anyone else. I obey the laws of Zarada, whatever they may be."

"But it doesn't make sense. Miran doesn't want to be Sultana, and she has no ambition, yet she will have the most powerful voice on the island. I do want that title, I have something to say and yet I will be voiceless. It's not fair. I'll be a nobody, living in a common cottage, scratching away for my living."

"Your words reveal your heart, my child. Being Sultana has nothing to do with power. There are many others whose voices must be heard and weighed when making decisions that affect us all. It's up to the Sultana to understand the wants of individuals as well as the needs of the whole community. These things you say, they wouldn't be influenced by your mother in any way, would they?"

Sultana Henrit could tell by the look on Anay's face that she didn't want to answer that question. She rose with difficulty, using her cane to help her walk around the room. She touched various objects: a bone, a rock, a sculpture. "What does power mean to you?" she asked.

Anay went to the window, aware of the dryness in her throat as she gazed out at the empty riverbed, the parched dirt that used to be filled with fresh water. "Controlling outcomes, making things go my way."

The Sultana joined Anay at the window, placing her hand on Anay's arm. She looked at the naive youth. "You have been misled. Being Sultana means giving up all aspirations, especially those of a personal nature."

"That's not what mother says."

The Sultana pointed to the mantle. "Do you see that photo of me? There I am, young and alive and full of ideals, just like you are now. Back then, I had my own concepts about how things should be."

Anay couldn't imagine her grandmother as anything but the shriveled old woman she saw before her. "That was different."

"Not so different. I wanted to change everything; the laws, the rules, the ways of this island. The High Council at the time was very old fashioned in my eyes."

"Tell me about my grandfather," Anay said.

The Sultana chuckled at a memory she hadn't conjured in a very long time. "I was married to a fool of a man chosen by my parents. He was supposed to rule with me, but he was only in the way. I convinced him to go with the Brotherhood on their adventures over the ocean. He was a big brute, built for the world of men, not for life in the castle. He didn't understand how to rule this island and he definitely lacked the know how to rule my heart."

"But weren't you lonely?"

"Oh, I was in love, but with someone else."

"Really? Who?"

"After Selexi was born, my husband left on an expedition. He died. Fell into the mouth of a tarwox. He wasn't the brightest star in the sky. So, I *was* alone and many times lonely. I gave up my desire for companionship and became married to my role as a leader when the man I secretly loved wedded another.

"It was painful at first, but in the long run it was right. I was the Sultana and my first obligation was to the people and the land. That was ultimately more important to me than my personal happiness. The High Council members were much older than I and they shared their wisdom with me. They stopped me from doing many silly things." She smiled softly.

"I was never one to abuse power, but I had ideas. So many new ideas—I was going to make everything better! They would tell me to take it easy; changes take time. The High Council even discussed finding me another husband so I would spend less time working. But I was determined to make being Sultana the cornerstone of my life. If I couldn't have the man I loved, I didn't want another."

Anay knew there was truth in what her grandmother said, but she was too concerned with her own fate to make any parallels with her life. Instead, she coldly pushed it out of her mind. Any threat to her momentum to gain the throne had to be treated like a deadly disease and, like a tumor, cut away with the knife of resolve.

A Grandmother's Warning

Selexi listened for sounds from her daughter's room. "Anay?" she called out. There was no response.

She knew what the silence meant. Every so often Anay would run to her grandmother, and have her head filled with all varieties of tall tales that confused her thinking and punctured her nerve.

Selexi threw on her cloak and went out into the palace corridor, racing through the familiar labyrinth of hallways so fast that she knocked down an attendant carrying a tray full of food. Leaving behind the mess and the clatter, she came to the Sultana's door, knocking loudly and pushing her way past Raina as soon as the door opened. Storming into the study, she startled Anay who, like a thief caught in the act, cried out, "Mother!"

Selexi frowned. "I knew it. What did you think you'd find here? All you'll hear are lies."

Anay avoided her mother's gaze, but the Sultana met Selexi's stare dead on. "*You* are the master of lies."

Raina rushed in, gesturing apologetically.

"It's alright, Raina."

Selexi's fury bore into Anay like a hot iron. "What garbage have you been fed this time?"

Anay shifted her weight back and forth. "I...just wanted to..."

"Tell her the good news?" Selexi interjected.

"I didn't get to that yet."

Selexi walked across the room, laid her hands on her daughter's shoulders and announced, "You are looking at our next Sultana."

The Sultana casually ran her fingers over a stone sculpture displayed on a high table. It had been a gift from the elves on Saron—a figure of a darpon made of azurial metal, smooth and cool to the touch. "So you discovered the challenge clause. I expected you would. Eventually."

"Of course I did. We apparently couldn't count on you to tell us about it."

"I will not allow you to challenge Miran," asserted the Sultana.

Selexi snickered. "You can't stop us. We all know that Anay is superior. It couldn't be more apparent. Miran is a sniveling, timid, poor excuse for a young warrior. It's obvious she has no ambition whatsoever. Have you seen her with her camion? She treats it like a pet, not a warrior's beast ready for battle." She waved her hand as if shooing away a biting insect. "She's soft, pathetic."

The Sultana leaned into her cane. "I have given my life to this island. I will not allow you to destroy all I have worked for."

"But Grandmother, Miran won't mind if I take over," interjected Anay. "She doesn't even want to be Sultana. She told me that herself."

"She might not want it now. But it is her birthright. The clause you're referring to was designed to keep the truly incapable from having to bear the responsibility of being the leader they cannot be. It was not created for petty squabbles. Miran is perfectly capable of ruling and so she will become the next Sultana. Being the best warrior is the least of the requirements for being a great Sultana. I was decent with a sword, but nothing more. She will grow into the rest, just as I did."

Selexi's anger rose. "If you take that position, you are betraying Anay."

Anay blanched. Could her grandmother abandon her so easily?

The Sultana shook her head. "You are turning Anay into a jealous, heartless brute like yourself. If you succeed, she will make nothing but enemies. Even if she were to become Sultana, she would not survive long. In a matter of a few moon cycles, she would be voted out. You forget that provision in our laws." Her energy waning, she limped back to her desk, slumped into the chair, and closed her eyes.

Anay, despite her unshakable determination to challenge Miran, still had a soft spot for her grandmother. "She's not feeling well, mother."

Selexi ignored her daughter. "Nonsense. Anay will work with the High Council…enough to satisfy them."

With effort, the Sultana opened her eyes again. "Being Sultana has always been determined by the law of nature. Nature cannot be defied."

"There are ways to manipulate nature," Selexi seethed.

The Sultana rang for Raina. Anay made a movement to go to her, but Selexi grabbed her by the arm and swiftly guided her out the door. Anay glanced back, torn; a part of her wanted to be with her grandmother, but it was her mother she had to please in order to get what she wanted.

Quest for Red Larimar Stones

As Head Elder, Dosha held the highest authority in the High Council, a lifelong appointment chosen by the Sultana. The islanders could start a petition if they disagreed with the Sultana's choice, but in Dosha's case that would never happen. She was highly respected and well-loved.

In the privacy of her room, Dosha sat on a violet canvas pillow, meditating before an altar. Incense plumes rose up around her in grey swirls and multiple candles burned, their flames still and steady. Beams of light projected out from her third eye into the middle of the room, slowly fading outward before being replaced by fresh beams. The pattern repeated as she softly chanted.

A knock at the door brought her out of meditation. Taking a deep breath, her eyes opened halfway. She drifted back into worldly reality. "Come in," she said.

A messenger entered and handed her a parchment roll. She read the note and was not pleased with its contents. A furrow formed on her forehead as she restrained her outrage. *That Selexi—causing trouble*

94

again. She has been a problem from the time she was a small child. And now she is threatening the well-being of the entire island.

There was nothing she could do. It was within Anay's rights to exercise the challenge clause. Dosha put on her robe and stepped into the hallway, joining the rest of the members who were also pouring out of their rooms and heading toward the Rotunda for the emergency meeting.

The High Council members took their places facing the dais where the Sultana's throne was situated. Selexi smugly relished the commotion she had created. Everyone appeared to be agitated as she had hoped they would be. Anay and Miran stood to the side, waiting.

The Sultana had mustered the energy to come and she made no attempt to hide her distaste. It was clearly expressed in her sour expression.

Dosha banged the gong to start the proceedings. "Selexi's daughter, Anay, is challenging Miran to the throne."

Hushed murmurs circulated the room.

Dosha continued. "The book of our foremothers indicates that the girls must embark upon a quest of the Sultana's choosing. Since we are facing certain starvation from the drought, the Sultana has decreed that the girls will travel to Saron to harvest red larimar stones so we can call the rain. They leave at sunrise in two days' time."

Selexi sprang to her feet, her fist raised in protest. "This is outrageous! There's no need to send them on a trip that dangerous. They can fulfill their quest right here on Zarada." She looked at her mother. "You wouldn't risk the life of your only granddaughter. Or would you?"

Dosha would not tolerate such an outburst. "Silence, Selexi! Sit down or you will be escorted from the room."

Selexi considered her options. She could make more noise, but she had little power over the High Council and less over her mother. She acquiesced, taking her seat, and silently brooded.

The Sultana spoke, her voice weak, her passion strong. "We will not survive beyond the next season without rain for our crops. If we do not procure stones soon, we will be forced to leave Zarada and there will be no inhabitants on the island left to rule. Miran and Anay are our last hope for replenishing the red larimar stones. They are both highly accomplished young warriors and capable of bringing back the stones. If they fail, so will we. If they succeed, we will have life again!"

Again, Selexi spoke out of turn. "I say let Miran go alone as a test of her abilities."

The Sultana remained firm. "You can't have it both ways, Selexi. If Anay wants to be Sultana, she has to prove herself as well."

Dosha addressed the High Council. "Who is for this quest?"

All High Council members said, "Aye!", except Selexi, who sat tight-lipped in stony silence.

Bajo read from a decree, "Miran and Anay will travel to Saron on separate sea vessels, each provided with a full crew and all the supplies needed. "If you both bring back ten stones, we will enter the second phase of the challenge, and the winner of that will be crowned Sultana of Zarada.

"And, so it is!" proclaimed Dosha as she rang the gong.

The High Council confirmed, "And, so it is!"

Under the Sea

Another scorching day seared and baked the parched island. Beyond the crystalline shore, two great slashes of sunlight brazed the expanse of ocean, long gold belts sparkling upon waves of blue satin. It seemed calm on the surface, but beneath the waves it was another matter.

Two vegetable harvesters rode darpons, quick-swimming blue sea animals that raced over the ocean waves. The riders rode them deep down, where the wild vegetable strands grew. The harvesters dipped beneath the waves, brandishing curved machetes, cutting the few remaining tufts of seaweed from their stalks. With full sacks, they buoyed up, bursting through the surface, leaping into the air. Then they rode over to the waiting boats, tossing the sacks in.

"There's not much left down there," remarked the first harvester.

"And, it's getting late," added the second, looking at the darkening sky. "We'd better head back."

The harvesters climbed into the boats and gestured to the darpons to return to their herd.

As they parked in the boat slip, a group of young boys took the heavy baskets, carrying them to the sorting house where they were emptied onto a sorting table. The tangled seaweed was pulled apart and unfolded and the strips were laid out in neat rows. Next they were placed on a belt that wove through a device that wrung the seawater out of the seaweed. The strips were then put onto drying racks. Once the leaves dried, they were used in soups, or crushed and sprinkled on any number of dishes.

The harvest room supervisor, Janal, inspected the yield, taking notes on the quality and quantity of the plants. She seemed worried. "It looks like we might be able to last one more moon cycle," she said grimly. "And then—" Her voice trailed off as the familiar sound of low singing seeped into the sorting house.

It was the men returning from sea. The men spent much of their time traveling to different destinations, dealing in commerce with races from distant lands. Famous for the weapons they made, Zaradian men were also great traders, commonly bringing home spices, herbs, and other supplies. This time they had also managed to obtain a small amount of grain, although it had been purchased at a high price. It might sustain them until the rain brought in crops.

The village had always been ruled and run by the women. It was the natural order of things. In times of war men and women combined forces to make a mighty army. The rest of the time, the women were in charge of daily life, entrusted by the men to make the best decisions for the island in their absence.

The girls looked up pleadingly at Janal. She knew what they wanted. "Okay, okay," she said. "Go ahead."

The sorters rushed out the door, clamoring with excitement.

"But only for a few minutes!" Janal shouted after them, grinning at their eagerness.

Women from all over the island had come to meet the men that had been gone; married women looked for their husbands, little girls were lifted high by their fathers, and young ladies were embraced by their budding romantic interests.

"All right, men," Kurad boomed. "Make good use of your time at home!" Satrah, his daughter, gave him a warm welcome before returning to the sorting hut.

The youngest boys came to greet their fathers, swinging their slingshots and joking around and dreaming of coming of age so they too could go on adventures with their fathers, brothers, uncles and grandfathers.

Anay scanned the crowd for Pallo. She didn't like him all that much, but many of the other girls had romances and she liked to keep up the image of having one too. She saw him and he made his way over to her. She noticed Grideon, Miran's intended husband, and tried to catch his eye but Grideon looked past Anay. He only had eyes for Miran.

Anay was deflated. Her jealousy bled into every aspect of Miran's life. She vowed to take back everything that would have been hers...that still could be hers.

She showed little enthusiasm when Pallo approached her. He was part of her old thinking—a consolation for what she couldn't have. Now she was angling for what she really wanted and deserved. Pallo wasn't part of that vision.

Miran jostled through the crowd searching for Grideon. She spotted him walking up the path talking with his friends and her heart melted, her face flush with happiness. Grideon came toward her, his arms open wide. She fell into his embrace, wrapping her arms behind him, burying her face in his neck, inhaling scents of salt air and canvas. "I've missed you," she sighed.

"Not as much as I've missed you."

Anay watched Miran and Grideon with disdain. She grabbed Pallo's hand roughly. "Let's get out of here."

"But I just got here," Pallo teased.

"Well, I'm going home to the castle," and with that she released his hand walked away.

Pallo watched her go, puzzled. Sometimes he didn't know what to make of her. She could act so strangely.

Grideon took Miran back to the sorting hut. "You're even more beautiful than I remember," he said, draping his hand around her waist and kissing her cheek.

Miran laughed. "How can that be? I am covered in sea vegetables."

"You're the most stunning sea creature I've ever seen. Maybe I should try," he cajoled, following her inside.

Janal looked up and shook her head. "No, Grideon. You can't be in here."

"But it smells so nice!" he said.

Janal laughed. "I mean it."

The girls in the hut stifled laughter.

He reached into a vat of the discarded, inedible parts of the seaweed and poured a bunch on his head, the ragged remnants draping across his face. "Now I look like I belong here."

"It's a good start," chided Miran.

Grideon pulled out more scraps, pushing the slimy pieces under his shirt and pants, letting them stick out. Miran dug her hands into the vat and piled some over her own head and the room filled with laughter.

"Hey! Stop that!" Janal ordered, but even she couldn't contain a smile.

Covered in green slime, Grideon raised his arms up and roared, "Rrraaaa!!" He pranced around the room like a crazed animal, chasing Miran. She ran and then turned, chasing him back, both of them growling and clawing.

Janal, having given up, laughed out loud.

Miran ran out of the hut, and Grideon went after her. All the way to the shore, pieces of sea vegetables fell to the ground, leaving a trail. At the water's edge the air was cooling and a warm breeze drifted in from the sea.

Gideon smoothed Miran's hair away from her face. She removed a string of seaweed from his hair. The soft light of the setting suns danced in the blue flecks of his amber eyes. He was the only part of becoming Sultana that felt right to her.

"Would you be with me if I didn't...?" She faltered. "Maybe it isn't fair of me to ask."

"I could never love anyone the way I love you," he said. "But I do see you as our next Sultana. I believe you are the one to lead us."

She looked away, doubt clouding her face.

He put his fingertips under her chin and turned her face back to his. He saw how worried she was. Taking her hands in his, he said, "I know you've been grappling with this a long time. If you decide not to become Sultana, I will also give up my claim as Sultan. We will have a beautiful life together no matter what because we know who we are."

Miran felt a wave of relief wash over her as Gideon leaned in and kissed her and for an exquisite moment she allowed herself to be free of the uncertainty of the future.

Anay's Deception

Miran was at home reviewing special procedures she needed to learn. Protocol specific to being Sultana. She had made plans to meet Grideon on the beach after putting in some solid hours of study.

Her work complete, she slipped into a black dress and jeweled sandals, then put on green stone earrings and matching necklace. She brushed her long hair until it shone, pinning it up with a shell comb.

Satisfied, she went out and made her way to meet Grideon at what she thought was the most romantic place on the island. It was their special spot. Looking up at the moons, she smiled at the promise of seeing him.

The Casbah Club was more raucous than usual. The more severe the drought became, the more frequently the villagers came to escape from their worries. There was still a supply of flower tea and grain ale in the storehouse, and they could at least fill the stomach with something.

In the sprawling club, tables overflowed with drinks, playing cards and piles of multicolored triangular chips. Glasses clinked and an occasional sound of breaking glass came from behind the bar. Trails of smoke rose from pipes held in players' hands or clenched in their teeth of gamblers aiming for a win. Loud voices and laughter rippled in waves from table to table while musicians banged out bawdy tunes in the corner.

Anay was at a table in the center of the room, holding a set of cards in her hand. She bet a few chips and was dealt another card. She bit her lip and glanced over at Grideon, making sure he was still there. Her mother had coached her on the plan. Tonight she would win him over. Tomorrow she would show the High Council that Miran wasn't desired by the intended Sultan. It just might cause the quest to Saron to be canceled. Or perhaps Miran would be intimidated into capitulating when she realized Grideon didn't love her.

She felt for the vial in her pocket. Gathering courage along with her winnings, she wandered over to Grideon, trying to act casual, as if it were the most natural thing in the world to take a seat next to him. Laying her chips on the table, she he laughed and joked, feigning conversation.

A few more rounds of card play went by with Anay feeling only frustration. Unless Grideon looked away or took a break, she wouldn't be able to do what she needed to do. Then her chance came; when the music stopped the players turned and clapped. With Grideon's back to her, she took the opportunity to pour the contents of the vial into his drink, an odorless powder her mother had concocted.

Grideon stretched his arms above his head and yawned. "I think I've had enough," he said, collecting his chips. "See you all later." He pushed his chair back.

"Wait," Anay said, gripping his forearm.

Annoyed, he pulled away.

She laughed. "I mean I haven't had a chance to beat you. Another round?"

"I'm meeting Miran. I have to go."

"Please. Give me just one more chance."

"Okay, fine. One more round. But you're not going to beat me." He pulled his chair back in and put the chips back on the table.

Anay raised her glass. "Here's to the winner." Clinking her glass against his, she watched him take a long swallow.

The cards were dealt. The players took their turns placing bets, folding, raising, winning and losing. Anay kept Grideon engaged by raising her bets higher than her cards warranted and encouraged him to drink by raising her glass to him. She extended the game by every clever trick she knew to keep him there as long as she could.

Grideon has consumed enough of the drink to feel the effects. Sweat collected on his brow as the poison entered his bloodstream. He felt dizzy, light-headed.

Anay laid her cards down. She had nothing. He looked at her with contempt. "Bluffing. Why am I not surprised?"

He guzzled the rest of his drink down. Now she could let him go. He slid his winnings off the table and headed to the cashier to exchange the chips into tira before leaving the stuffy club. The fresh night air felt good.

Anay bumped into him. "Oh. Grideon. Sorry, I didn't see you."

He grabbed the reigns of his camion. "Sure, you didn't."

"How much did you win tonight?"

Grideon wished she wouldn't talk to him. "Some," he replied.

Anay stroked his camion's neck. "You are so pretty," she cooed, provoking a loud purr.

"Miran's waiting for me. Come on, boy," he said gently, picking up the reins and walking away.

Anay followed him. "Of course, she is. But there's something I'd like to show you first; it won't take long."

He kept going, his gaze straight ahead. "Maybe some other time."

She ran ahead of him, blocking his path. "Anay—" he started. But before he could utter another word, she raised her wand and began chanting.

"Hey!" he cried. "You're not supposed to have one of those—" But it was too late. She was already putting a spell on him, mesmerizing him with circular

107

movements. He fell into a stupor. His mouth hung open, his eyelids drooped.

"Follow me," Anay softly commanded.

Anay went to the woods, walking along the path that led to the shore. When they reach the beach, it was deserted, the reflection of two half-moons shimmering on the water. She stood at an angle that would make her silhouette against the night sky captivating.

Grideon, having completely forgotten all about Miran, was drawn in by Anay's flowing hair and sparkling green eyes. Her very soul seemed to be calling out to him. He moved closer, wanting to touch her.

"Grideon, do you see how the moons glow? How stunning they are?"

"Yes, Anay."

She turned to him. "That's how you will see me from now on."

"Yes, Anay."

She pulled his arms around her waist. "Tell me how you see me."

Grideon, a dopy look on his face, intoned, "You are as the moon, beautiful and mysterious."

She brought him closer, her lips inches from his. "You are in love with me. You think only of me."

He leaned in, grinning sheepishly. "Only of you."

Anay grinned back. "Now, all we have to do is seal this spell, I mean this true love, with one little kiss."

"One little kiss."

"Kiss me. Now."

Grideon leaned in. Anay tilted her head back and closed her eyes.

Miran emerged from the woods. "Grideon! No!"

The sound of Miran's voice snapped Grideon out of his trance. He looked around, dazed. When he saw where he was and the position he was in, he stumbled away from Anay, confused. "How—how did I get here?"

Miran seethed at Anay. "What have you done to him?"

Anay ignored Miran. "Grideon, I love you as much as you love me. You know that, don't you? I wouldn't do anything to hurt you."

"But I love Miran," he said. "You tricked me. That's not love."

Anay crossed her arms. "Maybe you don't know it, but I was supposed to be the Sultana. You and I were supposed to be together. When I win the challenge, you will be mine."

Grideon shook his head in disbelief. "Never."

"The High Council will demand that you marry me, the next Sultana. It will be my right to choose."

Miran gasped. She turned and sprinted into the darkness.

Grideon chased her, calling out, "Miran!"

She raced along the shore, disappearing around a rocky bend. He ran after her until he caught up. She stood in the shadow of a boulder, her back to him, arms crossed.

"Miran…" he began.

She spun around. "Why don't you just go back to her? She's going to have you in the end, anyway."

"She must have spiked my drink," he explained. "I didn't know what I was doing. If I had known…I would never have…I'm so sorry."

As much as she wanted to hang on to her anger, Miran knew it wasn't his fault. "Since the announcement of the challenge, the pressure has been unbearable. Seeing you two together…if giving up the throne means losing you…"

"You'll never lose me," he reassured her.

"How can I know that for sure?"

Selexi's Deception

Selexi hunched over her laboratory table late into the night. All around the room, bottles bubbled with viscous slime, beakers overflowed with moldy growths and flasks sputtered and spewed dark murky distillations. Formulaic equations and complex charts hung haphazardly on the walls. In the corner, the mutant creatures lay in their cages, sleeping.

Earlier in the day, she had snuck into the High Council's office, stealing the maps created especially for each girl's route to Saron. She now threw them into a glass bowl and set them on fire. As they burned, she unfurled two identical rolls of parchment, these unmarked, and spread them flat on the table, anchoring them with flasks.

The two new maps looked exactly like the ones Dosha had created, except the routes hadn't been drawn in yet. She picked up a red pencil and traced the routes she wanted each ship to take. For Miran she outlined a difficult path through a stormy area, right into the territory of the tarwox. He could be counted on to finish her off! For Anay, she chose an easy path that would take her to the opposite side of Saron, avoiding the tarwox and the storms. There was more of a desert on that side, but Anay would survive a couple of days in that environment. It was better than the mountains Miran would have to traverse. She took a step back, admiring her handiwork, cackling at her furtiveness.

There was a knock—Anay's special rhythm. Selexi pressed a button and the door opened.

Anay, feeling deflated, went immediately to the cages. The mutants provided her with the only affection she had ever known. "What do I have for you today?" she asked the sad creatures as she pulled tasty morsels of beetles and grubs out of her pocket.

At the sound of Anay's voice, the mutants stirred. She doled out the treats, patting them on their heads, scratching them under their chins. She loved them all but had a special place in her heart for Shosi, the grey and white one. He had a sweet personality and a high intelligence. She had trained him to do a few tricks when her mother wasn't around. Selexi admonished her one day when Anay asked if she could take Shosi home. "These *things* can never be seen outside this room!" she said. "My secret would be out, and our future ruined. What a ridiculous notion!"

Selexi finished marking the maps and rolled them up. "Tell me what happened! Is Grideon yours?"

Anay picked Shosi up and held him close, not wanting to engage with her mother, fearing the wrath that was sure to follow.

Selexi yelled, "Tell me!"

Anay gathered her resolve. "I'm not going through with this challenge."

"What do you mean? Wasn't the spell effective? It was freshly made; it should have been potent. What did you do wrong this time?"

"No, I mean yes, it worked. And for a moment I thought I had him, but—

"But what?!"

"Miran showed up and broke the spell."

Selexi grimaced. "Aargh. Miran. It's always her, meddling in my plans."

"It's my fault. I took him to the place they always meet. So she would see us. See him, kissing me I mean. I shouldn't have taken him there."

Selexi remembered the maps. "Can't you outsmart her just once?"

"Maybe she's smarter than I am."

"Don't be ridiculous. That weakling? Smarter than you? Impossible. No matter. Once you are Sultana, Grideon will see Miran for who she is—just a common girl. He will love you in the end. You'll see."

"But...I don't know." Anay put Shosi back in his cage and twisted an end of her hair between her fingers. "He loves her."

Selexi went to her daughter, leaning in close. Anay could smell her rancid breath. "Now you listen to me. I have not worked this hard and waited this long to have

113

you back out now like a sniveling bondo. You are going to beat that little runt and marry Grideon."

Selexi picked up the rolls and held them high, punctuating the air with them. "Love! Love can't conquer *this*!" She pointed the maps at Anay. "Miran will die on this quest and then we will run this island the way we want to!"

Realizing what Selexi held in her hands, Anay's eyes widened. "You changed the routes?"

"Are you doubting my methods?"

"No. But—"

Selexi dismissed Anay's complaint by turning her attention to her experiments, her graphs, her computations. "You leave everything to me. I'm on the verge of a very important breakthrough that will ensure that all our dreams come true. Run along now. You have a quest to begin and I must continue my work."

The Quest Begins

The dense morning fog moved inland, damp pre-autumn coolness a welcome relief from the blazing rays of the summer months. The wind, high and strong, pulled in one misty layer after another, covering the island in blankets of grey.

Friends and family of the girls and many of the villagers were arriving to witness the departure of the young warriors on their great quest to save them from starvation. Soon a crowd had gathered on shore, including the men, who had not yet returned to sea.

The Sultana arrived in her carriage, eager to watch the departure. The High Council huddled near the water's edge, their ceremonial pale green robes billowing in the crisp wind, their faces somber in the ashen light. Cavalo and Otho reposed on the shore, their bellies on the sand, their giant feline eyes blinking lazily. Soon, they would be led onto the ships and taken to the hull where clean stalls awaited them. Beyond, the two ships rocked on the undulating waves.

Dosha raised her mallet and swung it down against the gong, the metallic sound hushing the onlookers and that was the signal to bring Miran and Anay in front of the High Council to receive their instructions.

Before she spoke, Dosha looked at the girls with a depth that reflected the seriousness of their mission. Then she began. "Miran and Anay, this is the beginning of a long and arduous journey and it will end in triumph, failure, or death. One of you has to procure at least ten stones for the rainmaking ceremony. Do not try to get more; their potency lasts only a short period and the extra time it could take might cost you your lives. Daemons await you on the summit. You must get past them twice; once on your way in, and a second time on your way out."

Thaya presented two small blue amulets filled with a murky brown liquid, each hanging from a tree-leather rope. She pulled one over Anay's head and the other over Miran's. "Your supply of transformational potion," she said. "Use it wisely."

Bajo handed each girl a roll of parchment. "These are the maps of the island itself, which you will need once you arrive. The captains have the route maps to get you to your starting point on Saron. Miran will land at the North end, Anay the South. They are equidistant from the summit where the stones grow, in the center of the island."

"Once you get to Saron, it is up to you to find your way to the field as you see fit. You must return to your vessels by the quarter moons waxing at the apex. After that time, the sea will be too dangerous to cross, leaving

116

you stranded on Saron until the tide changes back, many moon cycles from now."

Madeek stepped forward. "You are now to be given swords that can transform or kill." She pointed to the lever on one handle. "Yellow is transformation. Black is death. Use the black lever only as a last resort, but never on one another. That would constitute the highest of crimes."

They took the swords and slid them into their sheaths.

Dosha continued. "Using all your knowledge and wisdom to withstand the trials ahead of you will be essential to your chances of returning home safely. Be wise, be brave and be victorious. Remember, we are depending on you for our very survival. Now go."

Freya tugged at Miran's cloak. "Goodbye," she said, tears filling her eyes. Miran hugged her little sister.

Adean was reluctant to see her daughter depart. "I'm very proud of you—" Her voice choked off. "If you—"

"I'll be fine, Mother."

"Of course you will." She reached into her pocket and pulled out a pewter charm strung on a silver chain. Miran recognized it as the necklace her grandmother wore in the old photograph; the rain goddess with the piercing gaze and fiery hair and a red larimar stone at her heart. The charm was now tarnished, the crevices blackened by time, the pewter worn. The stone, however, was still bright and clear and shining.

117

Adean fastened the necklace around Miran's neck. "This belonged to your grandmother."

"The stone. It's…" Miran started.

"Yes, my darling. It's a red larimar."

"She wore this when she was young."

"Your grandmother, Galanee, was the last larimar hunter. After her disappearance, no one has had the courage to take her place. I found it amongst her things. She would have wanted you to have it."

Miran had been six when her grandmother disappeared. Her Mabu used to speak of things she wanted to hear about, weaving stories laden with adventure and wisdom. Whenever they were together, Miran had a heightened sense of reality that was a strong anchor in her small world. And now *she* was continuing the work of her grandmother. Miran let this sink in. *I am taking her place.*

The potential danger of her voyage was becoming clear. And now there was a deeper purpose; a responsibility to collect the stones in the name of the person she loved most.

Miran embraced Adean once more and when she turned away, Grideon was there waiting, flowers in hand, suddenly appearing fragile. It had always been he who left her behind when he went away on trading missions and expeditions. But there had always been a joyous sense of adventure to his departures and an anticipation of reuniting. This trip was different, bleak somehow. It might be the last time they ever saw each other.

He held her close and as she felt his strong arms around her, strength welled up inside her. This newfound confidence made her love Grideon even more ardently. She was convinced that he loved her, come what may, and fought the urge to take his hand right then and there and escape with him far up into the mountains; to shirk this responsibility and be the way they were before—innocent children, free of cares and full of wonder.

It was a nice daydream, but she couldn't abandon the quest—she had to go through with it. So, holding the flowers, she stepped into the rowboat with Satrah and let herself be pulled away from everything she knew and loved.

Cheering erupted as the girls made their way toward their ship. Musicians played happy tunes and there was hope in the air.

Selexi took Anay's shoulders firmly in her hands, relaying final instructions. "Stay focused and keep a sharp eye out. Don't trust anyone. And if you get a chance to impede Miran, take it. Take it and run and don't look back. Do you understand, child?"

Anay nodded. "Yes, Mother."

The horn sounded. Anay turned to go.

"Remember, it's all up to you!"

With this final charge, Anay boarded the rowboat.

119

Horns blasted. Anchors wound up with a grating clatter, freeing the ships to move out to sea. The crowd broke loose with fresh hoots, hollers and cheers. The musicians started up a farewell fanfare. Hats were thrown in the air, babies were kissed and the seeds of happiness were securely planted.

Miran and Satrah were standing at the railing when Astrielle flew up. "Leaving so soon?" she chirped.

Miran's face lit up. "I was hoping you would come and see me off!"

Astrielle alighted on the railing, giggling. "I was hoping you'd let me come along."

"Are you sure?" Miran asked. "It's going to be dangerous."

"Much too dangerous for a fairy," Satrah advised.

"Both of you will protect me," Astrielle answered.

Miran grinned. "Of course we will. Hop on!"

"I knew you would!" sang Astrielle.

Satrah teased. "Her fairy skills might come in handy."

"They most certainly will!" Astrielle sang.

Miran laughed, grateful that she wasn't alone.

The ship began to shift, slowly at first, then it picked up speed, briskly moving away from shore. Miran waved to her mother, Freya and Grideon, watched them shrink smaller and smaller until they merged with the mass of waving arms and finally the island was just a nebulous shape in the distance.

She closed her eyes and imagined herself diving off the deck of the ship, plunging below the surface. In the cold silence there would be sea vegetables dancing with the tide, fish darting back and forth. It would be peaceful there. She could find mermaids and live with them forever.

New sounds—rushing water, running footsteps, the clanking of gear and the scraping of crates—brought her out of her daydream. Deckhands scurried here and there while the captain barked out orders. Around her there was only boundless blue water, Zarada was gone.

She let the sounds fold into one another and gazed out into the distance, her hand clutching the pendant. She found comfort in the knowledge that it had belonged to her grandmother and it strengthened her resolve to find the courage she needed.

PART 2

Which Path to Take?

In the dining hall of the great ship, breakfast was served. Miran, Astrielle and Satrah sat at the end of a long table that was bolted to the floor. Astrielle had her own tiny plate, bowl, utensils and drinking cup. The crew sat in clusters. As they polished off the last of the stewed grains, one of the deckhands approached Miran. "The captain has requested your presence in the control room."

Miran gulped down the last of her tea. "Show us the way."

The floor swayed with the force of the waves and wind outside. Miran held tight to the railing, barely able to see where she was placing her feet in the dark and narrow stairway, slick with seawater. "You'd better hop in here," Miran said to Astrielle, pulling open the flap of her front pocket. "It's pretty rocky."

Astrielle jumped into the safe refuge.

As they reached the top, a thin strip of light glowed around the door, painting a yellow strip of light across Miran's cloak that traveled downward as she ascended.

When the door opened, their eyes were flooded with dazzling sunlight. Cool mist clung to their skin.

The sky was an umbrella of boundless blue, tufts of white skidding across it like skipping stones. It was noisy on deck; the crew was busy retying knots, shifting sails, loading and unloading crates and climbing impossibly high rope ladders.

Miran blinked several times, adjusting to the light. Satrah shielded her eyes with her hand and Astrielle squinted, taking in all the new sights and sounds.

Captain Tinnon was in an enclosed room on a higher level, shielded behind a thick pane of glass, a trail of smoke rising from her pipe as she waved to Miran and her friends, inviting them to come up and join her.

Brondi, the captain's first mate and an experienced seafarer, opened the door, a red scarf wrapped around her head, a brown tree-leather patch covering one eye. With her good eye, she sized them up.

"Come in!" Captain Tinnon bellowed with a wide smile. Her short grey hair was topped with a black canvas sea cap that balanced on her head like a lopsided cake. She clenched a pipe between her teeth and puffed on it several times, smoke fanning out in swirling shapes. The combined scents of pipe tobacco and sea salt hung in the air like thick perfume. "You are most welcome here," she said.

"We are grateful," Miran said. "These are my friends. Astrielle and Satrah."

"Very good," answered the Captain. "Excellent. Now, let's look at your map."

Brondi monitored dials on the console while the captain coaxed her pipe. She pinned the map on the wall and used a long wooden pointer to trace the route indicated on the map. "The route they have given us is treacherous," she said with one side of her mouth. "Your High Council told me I must stay on the path drawn here. But I can't take you this way. It's too risky, you see. We'll perish if we attempt it."

She studied the map further, chewing on the pipe, as if looking at it long enough would somehow provide an answer.

Miran sensed that something wasn't right. The High Council would never send her into a death trap, putting her mission to procure the stones in jeopardy. *It must have been tampered with.* "Selexi," she muttered under her breath.

Satrah understood immediately. "Of course."

"Oh dear," cried Astrielle, a pretty little hand covering her mouth.

"What's that you say?" asked Tinnon, cocking her head. "What is Selexi?"

Miran felt a bubble of rage inflating inside her, threatening to pop. *The idea is to get me out of the way. Selexi might be found out and punished. But by then her goal will be accomplished; I will be dead. She will endure the prison sentence and can direct Anay—who will likely still be appointed Sultana—from her cell.*

125

Anay can eventually pardon her mother with enough guile. So that is her plan!

She considered her options. If she took another route, would her quest be invalidated? There was no way of knowing what the High Council would do. She suddenly had the urge to beat both mother and daughter at their own game.

The thought of Selexi riled her anger and the anger transformed into determination, melding into a steely resolve. She met Captain Tinnon's worried expression with a hard look. "Selexi is not a 'what'. Selexi is a 'she'. And 'she' will be outsmarted. We will take the route on the map."

Tinnon was taken aback by the young warrior's fiery gaze. "But—you don't know what you're saying."

Brondi crossed her arms, her head shaking vigorously. "Be torn apart by the storms. Even if we survive the storms, there are tarwoxes."

"What are tarwoxes?" asked Astrielle.

Brondi's face paled. "Worse than your Selexi, I imagine. A tarwox is a sea monster that lives in Death Hollow. Been terrorizing seafaring travelers for as long as I can remember."

"It's suicide," Tinnon said, as she tapped the map with the pointer. "It *is* a more direct route and it appears we would arrive faster. But if it storms and we encounter a tarwox, we won't make it. It's that simple."

She pulled out a telescope and peered through it, moving the instrument from left to right, surveying the horizon. Then—something stopped her—a grey patch. "There's a mean storm brewing in that direction. If we go around the other way, we'll avoid trouble."

"We must follow this route," Miran insisted. "If I want to turn back, I'll let you know."

Tinnon exchanged a glance with Brondi. "Once we enter Death Hollow, there is no turning back."

"We can make it," Miran said. "I know we can."

Satrah was doubtful. "Are you sure you want to do this? You don't have to. It's a trap."

"I'm not sure I want to," Astrielle chimed in. "At all."

Miran was unwavering. "I'm sure," she said. "Absolutely."

"It's *your* quest and these are the orders," the Captain said. "We'll do what you say. Brondi—forge on."

And so they forged on. Night fell. Miran lay in her cot. Astrielle was curled up next to her and Satrah had taken the next cot over. They were both asleep. But Miran remained awake, doubting herself, wondering if she made the right decision. The storm had begun. The sound of pelting rain and the creaking of the ship made an eerie backdrop to the fear that enveloped her. She clutched the pendant, red indentations forming as the charm pressed deep into her skin.

Thoughts of failure circled her mind like hungry dokens. She grasped the pendant ever more tightly, her knuckles blanching white. Entering a fitful sleep, she dreamt of her lost Mabu, Voices broke through the silent darkness:

Miran...
Mabu?
I am waiting for you.
Where are you? How do I find you?
Over here, come closer.
Mabu...I can't see you.

Miran tossed and turned, mumbling, "Come back...Mabu...?"

Astrielle hovered over her friend, wings buzzing. "Miran, wake up. It's only a dream."

Satrah shook Miran by the shoulder. "Miran."

Miran's eyes fluttered open. "She's alive!" She climbed down from her cot and got dressed.

"Who?" Astrielle asked.

"My grandmother. She must still be on Saron." She threw on her clothes and moved toward the door.

"Where are you going?" Satrah asked.

"Whatever is coming, I want to be up there to help get us through this. We have to get to Saron."

"I'll come with you," Satrah said as she got dressed.

"Me, too!" Astrielle chirped, slipping into Miran's pocket.

The ship raced forward, splitting the chopping waves. Lightning flashed, casting a bewitching white glow across the turbulent sea. Sails flapped violently, straining the ropes. Behind them, a tarwox, unhindered by the storm, propelled itself toward the ship.

Brondi was pleased with the speed and was hopeful they could outrun a tarwox after all, but suddenly the ship slowed and struggled, whining and screeching like a wild animal caught in a trap. Something was wrong. The gears were running hot, grinding for release.

She knew what was happening and did what she could to steady the vessel. They had hit a dense patch of high growing sea vegetables. In normal circumstances, it would mean a short delay, with a diving team sent down to cut the tangled plants and free them to be on their way. But if a tarwox was near, it would be upon them before they could even get their diving gear on. Besides, it was night. The water torches would draw the creature like insects to a flame.

Indeed, there was a tarwox near and had been following the ship for some time. It took notice of the whining, its limited brain interpreting the sound as a sign of prey growing tired. Coming up for air, it raised its ghastly head into the air, a long deep howl echoing into the blackness, before sinking down and swimming with renewed vigor toward its victim.

The howl reverberated throughout the ship, rousing the captain from her slumber. She sprang out of bed and pulled the emergency whistle. Hearing the alarm, the crew rolled out of their cots and hurried into their rain gear, scrambling onto the deck for instructions. The camions, locked inside stalls down below, pawed at the doors, growling restlessly.

Brondi checked the gauge again. It was pushed to the limit. She tried in vain to back out.

Tinnon burst into the control room. "Take her out!"

"I'm trying to, but we're in a tangle! Stuck in the sea vegetables!"

Miran and her friends arrived on deck to the pandemonium of the crew preparing for an attack. Seconds later, a strike hit the side of the ship. The beast was upon them. In a second, the flooring beneath them seemed to slide away and Miran was thrown down. She braced herself with her hands and knees, hitting the deck hard. Splintered wood penetrated her skin.

The captain gave orders. "We don't have time to untangle her. We'll have to subdue the creature."

The captain gave orders to the crew. They secured cargo and unloaded supplies as another thump rattled the ship, shaking them off their balance. Miran and Satrah, rain streaming down their faces, held tight to the railing.

The captain's voice cut through the sounds of the storm. "Fanna, Kartha, ready the catapults! Everyone else grab any rope you can find to secure yourselves!"

Another blow shocked them as coils of rope were distributed.

Miran looked over the railing, taking in the sight of the enormous beast. The stench of rotting fish mixed with rusted wet metal rose from its discolored grey skin.

Thick bumpy scales oozing with green slime covered its back. As the water flowed and receded, its large nostrils flapped open and shut, its yellow eyes remaining open while its short pointed ears flattened against the sides of its head. A blunt growth, perfectly designed for ramming, protruded from the top of its head.

Grunting noisily, the tarwox took stock of the morsels above, pangs of hunger rippling through its belly. It dove below, taking aim for the boat again.

"Here it comes!" Tinnon shouted. "Hang on!"

The creature struck again. Some on deck were lifted off their feet by the force of the blow; others were knocked over.

Miran slammed into a pile of crates, a burning sensation shooting through her ribs. Astrielle was dislodged from her pocket, but the little fairy held tight to the lip of it and was able to climb back in. Satrah, having fallen, was getting back on her feet.

A deckhand tied an end of rope to the boat, then to her own waist, throwing the rest their way. Miran and Satrah started securing themselves with the rope.

"Not too long!" shouted the deckhand.

Miran shortened the length of hers. "What does it want?!" she asked, the roar of the thunder and crash of the waves muffling her voice.

"To eat, of course!" came the reply.

"What does it eat?!" asked Satrah.

"Anything, everything. It's insatiable!" A haunted look passed over the deckhand's face. "It likes to hit the

131

vessel hard enough to send us flying over the side and right down into its open gullet. Like a little treat."

"I don't like this at all," said Astrielle, shuddering from cold and fright. "I don't want to be a treat."

Miran felt a wave of fear pass over her, followed by guilt. But there wasn't time to indulge anything now except the courage she aspired to.

The tarwox was busy cracking the hull; planks were beginning to give way. The crew prepared three large catapults, stabilizing them with bags of sand. They had them loaded and were waiting for orders when suddenly the barrage of attacks stopped and all was quiet.

"What's happening?" Miran shouted over the howling wind.

Lightning painted pointed shards of white down the horizon and thunder cried out a deep rumble that shook the very stars. The deckhand squinted as the rain drizzled down her frightened face. "It's about to puncture the ship right through. But it wants to create a nice distance between us first so it can do the most damage."

They rocked and waited as the rain coated their faces and seeped into their clothing. Miran shivered. Her face shone with a ghostly pallor in the flash of lightning.

The captain raised her arm. Lowering it quickly, she cried, "Fire!"

The cannonball, covered in razor-sharp blades, flew through the air, but missed the mark, hitting the water instead.

The beast crushed its head against the ship and one of the crew was tossed high, rope and all. The creature rose up, bared its gruesome head and opened its jaws wide, grunting for its reward.

The girl fell straight into its mouth, swallowed down in one bite. The tarwox pulled the rope taut as he sank into the water. The rope shook and snapped up, flapping over the railing where it had been. It hung there tattered and bloody, fluttering in the wind.

"Are you okay?" Satrah asked Miran.

Miran gripped the rope that tied her to the ship, wishing she could turn back time. *The poor girl.* She nodded to Satrah, unable to find words.

The captain's voice pierced the air. "Fire!" she commanded, prompting the crew to fire a new slew of poisoned darts at the monster. They pierced its back and the tarwox surged up, towering over the boat, its hideous mouth grimacing in pain.

Miran agonized over the turn of events. *I have to do something.*

Astrielle watched in horror as Miran untied her rope, pulled out her sword and moved toward the creature.

"No Miran!" shrieked Astrielle.

Miran put Astrielle in Satrah's pocket. "Stay here," she said.

Satrah grabbed her by the arm. "Don't risk your life now. You can't bring her back."

"I have to do this. We're here because of me." Miran shook loose from Satrah's grip and continued toward the beast.

Catapults continued to fly, some missing, some hitting and injuring the tarwox, but it wasn't enough to stop the onslaught of barrages.

"What are you doing?!" the captain screamed at Miran. "I order you to move back. Immediately!" The captain gripped the railing, blinking against the rain. She felt a responsibility to get Miran to Saron. That was her task and here she was, watching her charge walk straight into the mouth of a tarwox.

"Help me beat it!" Miran shouted back.

Tinnon reluctantly signaled her crew to taunt the creature, drawing its attention away from Miran, who climbed the pole ladder closest to the tarwox.

The wind howled and gusted anew. A crack had opened at the bottom of the pole and as Miran climbed, she felt herself bouncing precariously, her weight making the crack widen further. Leaning over to test her range, her shoes slipped on the wet rungs and she almost fell. Shaking them off, she found better balance with bare feet. Suddenly a rope snapped and the crack in the pole opened wide, bringing her dangerously close to the tarwox who heard the crack and turned toward her. Once it saw Miran, it moved to snatch her from her perch.

134

Miran gripped the ladder with one hand and stretched her sword toward the beast with the other. She waited for it to attack, hoping she didn't fall into the sea.

The tarwox descended into the water and Miran didn't know where it might emerge. Her eyes darted around, frantically looking for it. In a great gush of water, it rose up, jaws opened wide, moving straight for her.

It was so sure of grasping her, it went in for the kill with complete abandon. The pole was still attached to the ship, but only barely. One wrong move and she would drop to her death. Suspended on the teetering pole ready to snap, her body was surrounded by the teeth of the monster. Its rancid teeth, just inches from Miran's face, were so foul she had to hold her breath. She kept the sword steady and as the deathly jaws closed around her, she touched the tarwox with the tip of her sword, freezing it in midair, encapsulating it in a swirl of paralyzing light.

The crew watched in utter amazement. When they realized what had happened, they broke into cheers. Miran turned her head to bask in the glow of her success.

"Well done, Miran!" the captain shouted.

"Turn it into a little teroid!" called a deckhand.

"A tree climber!" chimed in another.

"How about a fizard!" said yet another.

"Kill it!" ordered the Captain. "It will only transform back later and finish us off another rotten day."

Miran moved the lever from yellow to black, reciting the spell she had learned—the spell to kill the imprisoned opponent. A guttural sound emanated from the tarwox, low and raspy. It turned to a vacuous shell, first cracking and breaking into tiny fragments, then dust. The tarwox was gone.

Selexi's Difficult Decision

Selexi's latest creation—a combination of magik and biology—was her finest mutant yet. After many failed attempts, she was finally making progress. Once it was perfected, she planned to make thousands of them; then Zarada would be hers. This latest version was the closest she had come to what she had envisioned. Small and impish, with red eyes, pointed ears and a thin mouth, with a thumb and three fingers on each hand, ending in claws.

Tonight was the first time it had obeyed her commands, and this sent her into a frenzy of dark delight. She danced about the room, cackling. Sensing a presence, she stopped in mid cackle. Something or someone was lurking in the shadows. "Who's there?" she called out. "Show yourself."

From a dark corner, a tall and wiry thin being emerged. It was Arcodi, the Dictator of Vinda. Her metallic skin was varied in shades of blue and silver, the surface of it rippling like waves. Narrowly slanting eyelids framed eye sockets filled with fire. The top of her long oval head sprouted wire hair—shimmering, wild and kinky. She wore a tight black bodysuit and gleaming silver boots. She towered over Selexi, radiating cold brutality.

Selexi was not happy to see this visitor. She watched with irritation as the Vindan leader strode around the room, scrutinizing the experiments. "I haven't heard from you for some time," Arcodi accused.

"Nor I you," Selexi responded acidly.

Arcodi's eyes narrowed. "What have you been doing down here in your laboratory all this time? I demand to know."

"Nothing that would interest you."

Arcodi raised her fist. "Liar!"

"If you must know, I have just about finished it."

Arcodi dipped her finger into a jar of blue gel. She held it up to her eye and shot a flame out at the gel. "You must finish more quickly." The gel burned away. "Life is not good on our Island of Vinda. We are wanting for food, water and other supplies. Our island is very dry, very hot and very useless. We want this island back!" She banged her fist on the table and the gel spilled over the lip of the jar, onto the table.

"You cut down all the trees, so what do you expect?" Selexi admonished.

Enraged, Arcodi shot a ball of fire from her right eye into Selexi's hair, then brushed the jar of gel aside where it crashed to the floor, shattering. The globs of gel, as if magnetized, moved toward one another until they were one big glob. Selexi rushed to the sink and

138

turned on the faucet, dousing the flames under the water. She was boiling with rage but said nothing.

"Watch your tongue, or I will gladly remove it," said Arcodi. "Besides...I hear that you are suffering a drought as well, even with all your precious trees. Ran out of red larimar stones I suppose. That's a pity—for you. But it needs to be resolved before we live here. We must have rain."

"Why have you come so soon?" Selexi asked, drying her hair with a towel. "It's not ready yet."

Arcodi ignore the question. "My grandfather sold Zarada to your Sultana in a moment of desperation. We always intended to buy the island back. But your Sultana refuses to negotiate with us. We can't wait any longer. We will invade soon and take Zarada back by force, with or without you."

Selexi was on shaky ground. She couldn't build her army on Zarada. She was counting on Idocra to let her build them on Vinda. If the Vindans invaded before then, she could end up just like every other Zaradian. The Vindans would probably never be victorious, of course, unless they teamed up with another race. But they could do a tremendous amount of damage and throw her plan into a tailspin.

If that happened, her army may never be built. On top of that, Arcodi knew where her laboratory was. She could have it destroyed.

Arcodi's eyes landed on the new mutant. "I see our little project is coming along nicely. What do you call it?"

"It's a keru." Selexi lifted the keru and put it into its cage, locking it in. "It can be very dangerous."

Arcodi leaned down to take a closer look, wrapping her long fingers around the cage. She frowned. "I have a suspicion that you have your own plans for ruling this island with these kerus that don't involve us."

"Of course I intend to involve you."

Arcodi smiled crookedly. "With an army of these, we can reclaim the island. I will be able to arrange a place for you in the circle of power…if you cooperate and stick to the agreement."

"And if I don't?" asked Selexi.

"You will be run off the island or put to use as a slave, like the rest of the fools squatting here. Our army may not be made of great fighters, but we have other ways of controlling your kind." Arcodi stood at her full height, her large eyes bright and burning with dancing yellow flames.

Selexi considered her options. On their own, the Vindans would likely be beaten by the Zaradian army. But likewise, on her own, she may not be able to take control either, especially with only the small number of kerus she could amass here. The Vindans would wait for the kerus if she joined forces with them. She needed to buy time.

She would play along for now. But ultimately, she needed find a way to destroy the Vindans and reign supreme.

The Isle of Saron

Repairs made, the ship sped through the water while darkness stole the sea and hid it from everything but the moon. Saron was not far off now.

Astrielle slept in the nook of Miran's elbow. All the excitement had made her very, very tired.

Miran dozed off, drifting in and out of dreams.

The air is bright, milky and viscous. Miran looks down, her body is translucent. She looks back up. Her grandmother is floating before her.

"Miran..."

"Mabu?" Miran's throat rasps.

"I have been waiting for you," says her grandmother.

"Where have you been?" calls Miran. "I've been looking for you."

Her grandmother fades and drift away, then reappears.

"I'm always with you..."

Miran watches helplessly as the vision fades.
"Grandmother...don't go. Don't leave me."

Astrielle whirred around her sleeping friend. "Miran," she whispered. "Wake up. You're only dreaming again."

Miran's head turned from side to side. "Don't go...come back." She muttered something else, and then her eyes snapped open.

"What is it?" asked Satrah.

"Mabu." Miran rubbed her thumb against the cool stone in the pendant. "She said she's waiting for me."

"Waiting where?" Astrielle asked.

Satrah didn't want Miran to get her hopes up. "If she was alive, wouldn't she have found her way back to Zarada by now?"

Miran sighed. "Am I hoping for the impossible?"

A burst of voices filtered down from the deck, one louder than the others. "Land! The Isle of Saron!"

Satrah smiled. "We made it."

Astrielle buzzed about, chirping, "We made it! We're here!"

Miran and Satrah bolted up the stairs, Astrielle fluttering close behind. They opened the door to a glorious day—calm and warm and swathed in sunlight.

The captain passed the telescope around. Miran held the eyepiece up and saw a small blotch. Suddenly, an object obscured her view. She pulled the instrument away and a dazzling blue doken flew by. It rose up and circled the ship several times before landing on a sail pole, letting out a shrill "Squawk!"

Captain Tinnon chuckled. "Must be the welcoming committee!"

Elves

"There it is," Miran said, pointing. "The place where Mabu might have landed when she came to harvest stones."

Astrielle sat on the edge of the railing. She flew up to get a better view. "Oh, it's lovely!" she exclaimed, clasping her hands together. "This is a grand adventure!"

"The sand!" Satrah remarked. "It's grey! And, the trees are a strange shade of green—everything is different."

A soft breeze ruffled the sails as the anchor unfurled downward, breaking the silence. The crew stocked a lifeboat with supplies then lowered it into the water. A second boat was prepared for the travelers. The camions were released directly into the sea and swam to the beach on their own.

So much of the journey had seemed like a dream to Miran, but the sound of the lifeboat sliding over the sand as they skidded onto the beach made it very real. *If I made it this far,* she thought, *I might actually have a chance to get the stones. Dare I hope to find Mabu?*

145

The beach was covered in light grey sand dotted with tiny black shells. The shore merged into black soil from which lush, green foliage sprang up. There was a trailhead that led into what seemed to be a thick, dark jungle.

Miran stumbled a bit, the sway of the ship still in her legs, but it felt good to be back on solid ground. Brondi unloaded the supplies—food, water and camping gear—setting them down on the warm sand while Satrah loaded up the camions' saddlebags.

Tinnon, lighthearted for a change, smiled at Miran. "Thought we might not make it, eh? If it weren't for you, we wouldn't be here."

Miran shook her head. "If it weren't for me, you'd have gotten here without risking lives, or losing one."

Tinnon winked. "But that bloody beast would still be lurking out there and you might have lost the challenge."

"You were very brave," Brondi added.

Tinnon took off her cap, fluffing it up. "I expect you to be here when I arrive to take you home."

"I'll do my best."

"Why of course you'll be here!" Tinnon laughed heartily, flipping the cap on her head. "If you can kill a tarwox, you can grab a few stones from those brainless daemons! Ha!"

Miran laughed. "I hope you're right."

The captain's mood darkened "We have a delivery to make a few islands down the way. We'll circle back to get you in three days' time. If you're not here by the time the moons rise, we'll have to leave without you. Storms get too rough after that, and we can't risk being stranded. But I know you'll be here. So, be here."

"I'll be here."

"Me, too!" echoed Astrielle. "I'll be right here!"

Tinnon's smile returned. "Well, good luck to you and all that!" Securing her hat, she climbed into one of the rowboats. Brondi waved as she climbed into the other one and they went back to the ship.

Miran unrolled her map. It was time to figure out how to get to the summit. Satrah pulled out a pencil and they discussed which path was best, drawing the route they liked. They decided to head straight back from the coast for a few miles. That would bring them to the mountain range, which hopefully wasn't too hard to climb.

The blue doken reappeared, circling overhead, squawking.

Miran called up to it, "Hey, it's that doken again."

The doken cawed again, then disappeared behind the trees.

"Are we ready?" Miran asked.

"I'm ready!" Astrielle said, settling into a cozy spot on Cavalo's head.

Satrah tipped her head toward Otho and Cavalo. "Their load is pretty heavy," she said. "Might be better if we start on foot."

Astrielle addressed Cavalo. "I'm not heavy, am I boy?"

Cavalo snuffled.

Once in the jungle, away from the cool breeze that came off the water, the air was warmer and drier. The dense leaves made a tunnel of sorts; sometimes low and dark, sometimes high, with more light filtering in, patches of sky visible above them. At other times the path became so narrow they had to break branches and slash at the overgrown thicket with their daggers to get through.

At last the jungle ended, opening to a lush valley. Flocks of colorful birds cascaded through the air. Small mammals scurried and hopped along the ground. Wild animals—herds of bizarre beasts—grazed tranquilly, their tails swatting insects away.

They walked through the valley for a while, setting up camp at dusk and bedding down for the night, taking turns being on watch.

The next day they continued their journey. In the afternoon, they encountered a long stone bridge that went over a gulley. It twisted and turned, the far side of it taking them to the base of the mountain.

When they got to the mountain, Miran pulled out the map. "We should be able to get to the top by the end of the day," she said.

Satrah nodded. "And, tomorrow, the summit."

"Right." Miran rolled up the map. "Up we go!"

They continued on, climbing for some time. Astrielle made herself comfortable in the cushion of Cavalo's soft fur, at times sitting, other times lying down and sleeping.

As they climbed into higher altitudes, the greenery receded and the terrain grew rockier. The camions had trouble navigating around some of the more jagged rocks.

The doken appeared from time to time, cawing down at them. "Strange bird," said Satrah. "It's definitely trailing us. I've never seen a doken behave like that."

"I haven't seen any other dokens here at all," added Miran. "Maybe it's lost."

"Could be."

In the distance, the sound of rushing water beckoned them. Soon they found the source—a wide riverbank with quick rapids. Satrah walked up and down the riverbank in an attempt to locate a better crossing point, but she couldn't find one. They would have to cross on the camions.

They slowly guided their camions into the torrent of rushing water. Once in, it was relatively easy going, except for a few stumbles on the slippery stones. Once they reached the other side, Miran and Satrah led their camions up to a flat, open area. The camions shook the water out of their fur and began cleaning themselves.

"I'm famished!" Astrielle announced, waking up and stretching her arms.

Satrah said, "But you haven't done anything to build up an appetite!"

"I have a fast metabolism," Astrielle answered.

"Really?" Satrah said, laughing. "Well, then. Let's eat."

Miran and Satrah built a cooking fire and prepared a simple meal of boiled grains and canned vegetables. The smell of food made Miran realize how hungry she was. Satrah handed her a bowl filled with the first sustenance she had had in many hours. She devoured it with vigor, savoring each bite. "We need to keep moving," she said. "We have to make it to the summit by tomorrow, sundown."

Satrah nodded. "The camions need a rest and then we can go on."

"I'm ready whenever you are!" exclaimed Astrielle. "I don't need a rest."

Miran laughed. "Easy for you to say! You're riding in style."

"This whole trip has been one long rest for you," Satrah teased.

"There *are* advantages to being small," chirped the little fairy, as she held out her bowl for more. Satrah spooned out a fairy-sized portion. "You are good for the spirit."

Astrielle giggled. "And you are good for the taste buds."

After a short nap in the cool grass, they set off again, reaching the mountain peak at sundown. It turned out to be more of a mesa than a peak. On the far side, the mountain didn't decline gently as it did on the first side. It ended in a steep cliff, as if the top of the mountain had been cut in half vertically, the second half removed. There was only one way to get down—fly. They stood on the edge of the cliff, taking in the view of valleys and mountain ranges. Astrielle flew, hovering beyond the edge. Directly below, smoke rose up from a cluster of dwellings, the faint sounds of voices and music trailing up.

"Is that a village of some kind?" Satrah asked.

"I've heard mention of the elves of Saron," said Miran.

"Elves! Oh, we must go!" remarked Astrielle. "I've always wanted to meet elves."

Satrah looked at the map. "But the summit is in the other direction."

"We won't make it all the way to the summit before sundown. We've gone far enough for today. Besides, I want to ask the elves about Mabu—if they've seen her. Let's head down."

"Hurray!" exclaimed Astrielle, buzzing her wings with delight. "We're going to see the elves!"

Mounting their camions, they doubled back a good distance. Then galloping across the mesa, they leaped off the cliff, coasting down to the elf village below.

Findy the Harbinger

The afternoon heat was beginning to abate and the air cooled. They landed on the outskirts of the village and followed a narrow dirt road, traveling in the direction of the unsuspecting elves, whose voices and music grew louder and louder. They arrived to a charming scene: elf mothers hanging miniature laundry, tiny elf children running and laughing down the lane, shop owners selling their wares in an open market.

The elves were a happy and boisterous bunch, but as soon as the surprise guests were noticed, the terrified elves dropped what they were doing, scattering in every direction, urging each other to safety, alerting one another:

"Giants!"

"Monsters!"

"Quick, get inside!"

Miran called out to them, "Don't go, we just want to talk to you!" Her voice was drowned out amidst the ruckus of screeching and screaming and scurrying.

It was astounding how briskly they disappeared—quickly vanishing into their huts—slamming the doors and shutters tightly, locking them up—*clickety-clack*.

In a few moments, not a single elf could be seen nor heard. Only the faint sound of a baby's cry permeated the dusk air.

"Oh, the poor dears," lamented Astrielle. "They are frightened—of us!" She giggled.

Satrah was amused.

"Should I say something?" Miran asked her.

Satrah chuckled. "Sure, give it a try."

Miran cleared her throat. "Hello…"

"Louder," encouraged Astrielle.

Miran took a deep breath. "Hello! I'm Miran from the Island of Zarada! These are my friends Satrah and Astrielle!" She paused.

"Go on," cajoled Satrah.

"We are young warriors but we come as friends. You don't need to fear us. We'd like to meet you. We won't hurt you!"

A door handle jiggled, followed by the swinging open of the door. A red headed swaggering elf with a big smile on his rosy face emerged. Behind him was a four-legged animal, its body covered in pearly iridescent scales, its legs and paws a fluff of grey fur and out of its canine head— a plume of white feathers.

It was only a short distance, but the elf mounted his motley steed and rode it as if he were a royal king making an impressive entrance at an important event.

As if on cue, a troop of musicians came clamoring out, playing a lively tune to accompany the procession, milking every ounce of dramatic effect. When he reached the warriors, the elf came to an elegant halt, cued the musicians to stop and said, "Young warriors from Zarada. I am Findy, the Village Harbinger, I am. This is my trusty steed, Beast, he is." He smiled and tipped his hat proudly. "Welcome! What business have you here, so far from home?"

Miran said, "We've traveled here to harvest red larimar stones."

"Red larimar stones…well, well. That's an easy task, it is!" Snickers escaped from some of the huts.

"I'm also looking for my grandmother," Miran continued. "She was our stone hunter and was stranded here."

"Ahh, your grandmother…that's easy too. We've hidden her in the litchen pen, we have." He scratched his beard and consulted Beast. "Or did we put her up in the attic? I can't remember." Beast panted happily as Findy patted him on the head. More giggling seeped out of the huts.

"What's a litchen?" Astrielle asked.

"Ha! What's a litchen? I'll show you!"

Findy ran off behind his hut and came out carrying a funny little bird that clucked noisily. "These charmers give us our eggs, they do," he said proudly.

"Please," implored Miran. "We are suffering a terrible drought. Galanee, my grandmother, was our

154

stone hunter and, well, she's been missing a long time. Have you seen her?"

Findy looked at the closed-up domiciles and shouted out, "Has anyone seen this warrior's grandmother?"

A set of white shutters opened and an elf moved into view, his high-pitched voice pealing out, "Haven't seen none like her."

Findy scratched his beard, thinking. "I can take you to the Chief, I can. If anyone knows something, it would be him."

"We would be grateful. Lead the way," said Miran.

"Follow me," Findy said as he began down the road, shouting to the villagers, "You can come out now! We're on our way to the Chief and he'll want to hear how nicely we treated our guests! There's even a fairy amongst them, there is!"

Findy cupped a hand around his mouth and whispered up to Miran, "It might help if you come down from those giant whatever you call them."

Miran leaned over and cupped a hand over her mouth, whispering back, "Camions."

A window on the second floor of a hut slid open ever so slightly. A black bearded elf holding a tiny pipe peered through the opening, sending out a puff of smoke in salutation. A door from another hut creaked open and a woman, balancing an adorable elf baby on her hip, stood in the doorway, staring hesitantly. Others shyly ventured out to see the visitors more closely and soon the sides of the road were lined with a multitude of curious, rosy cheeked, bright-eyed elves.

Findy led them up the road and as they passed by, he placed his hands around his mouth and shouted, "Young warriors are here! Welcome them!"

The musicians started their happy tunes again. Miran and Satrah led their camions by the reins while Astrielle, excited to see elves, flew here and there, chirping to them, "Hello," and "Nice to meet you," and all the other niceties she could think of.

Miran and Satrah waved and smiled as they walked along, as if they were the main attraction in a grand parade. Little elf children looked up in amazement as the foreigners passed by with the longest strides they had ever seen.

One child in particular caught Satrah's eye. She knelt down and winked at him. When she stood back up, he ran between her legs, which made her laugh heartily. This was final assurance to the elves that these visitors were indeed friendly.

As they left the town, the sounds of the villagers faded away, and in a few minutes, they reached the compound of the Elf Chief. They knocked on the door and the Chief's wife opened it.

She looked up and, recognizing their origins, exclaimed, "Warriors! From Zarada!"

Findy nodded. "It's true!"

"How wonderful!"

Without needing any explanation, the Chief declared Miran and her friends honored guests. Since the warriors could not fit through the doorway, he ordered a feast for the road-weary travelers to be served outside in the courtyard. As they gathered around a small blazing fire, dish after dish of delicious elf food was served.

Miran, eating heartily, asked, "Do you have any advice on how to get the stones?"

"It's quite an undertaking," said the Chief. "Highly risky."

The Chief's wife nodded. "Very dangerous. And you're so very young. There is no safe way, I'm afraid. The daemons, you know."

"Yes, I'm aware of them. I'm also trying to find my grandmother Galanee, the great stone hunter. She disappeared on this island many years ago."

The Elf Chief's eyes lit up. "Galanee?"

"Yes."

"Of course we know her! She used to stop by and visit us. Her bag was empty on the way up, and full of red sparkling jewels on the way down."

The Chief's wife said, "One year she went up, but didn't return. We never saw her again. We wondered what happened to her."

Miran dug the heel of her boot into the ground, rotating it back and forth. "Then the daemons really did kill her."

"Maybe you shouldn't go to the summit, dear," the Chief's wife said. "We would hate to see you disappear, too."

"I have to go," said Miran. "It's part of my quest."

The Chief cleared his throat. "If you must go to the summit, take Findy with you. He knows this island better than anyone."

"Glad to be of service, I am," Findy said.

Miran mustered a smile of appreciation but couldn't bring herself to talk anymore. She was choking on her grief. Rising abruptly, she turned and left the Chief's compound and broke into a run. She came upon a group of elves dancing around a bonfire and sped past them in a blur.

Stepping off the main path, she wandered deeper into the jungle, her boots crunching against the dead leaves underfoot, her anger rising. Every step was an attempt to stamp out the frustration and pain that was enveloping her. She had reserved hope all these years that her grandmother was still alive. But it had been the hope of a child. She knew better now. The time for childish dreams was over.

She ran and ran until, breathless, she came to the edge of a pristine lake, still and glassy. The reflections of the moons shimmered on the smooth pane of the surface, pressing down like the heavy weight of sorrow that pressed against her heart. She picked up a handful of cool stones and drove them one by one into the water, breaking the reflection into pieces.

The Mysterious Doken

The next day, they woke up early. The elves packed them a basket of food to take on their journey and Findy led the way out of the village, taking a path that followed a winding river. He and Beast trotted along in front, enjoying a delightful conversation with Astrielle, who zoomed alongside until she grew tired. She then took a seat on Beast's head. Satrah and Otho were behind them while Miran, quiet and pensive, lagged at a distance.

Miran was still perplexed by the blue doken, who fluttered in and out of view. It did not display the typical behavior and habits of a doken. They usually went about their business without interacting with warriors. They weren't hunted but had a healthy fear of larger species. This one was definitely shadowing them.

Satrah shouted to Miran, "How are you doing back there?"

"That doken is still tracking us."

"Tracking *you*, you mean."

"Why do you say that?"

"It's always looking at you."

160

"Maybe it's hungry."

"I don't know. Dokens don't usually come to us for food."

"Well, what else could it want?"

Findy broke in. "Be careful about giving it anything. If it does take to your food, we might never be rid of the pest, we won't."

They rode all day and at dusk set up camp in a clearing bordered by large boulders and fallen logs. Firewood was gathered and a fire lit. They prepared a meal and fashioned seats out of logs they positioned around the fire.

The doken landed on a branch near Miran, silently studying her. Miran studied the bird while she ate. The doken cocked its head, adjusting its perch.

Miran got up and placed a morsel of food on a rock and took a step back. The doken descended from the tree and grabbed it. Instead of eating it, it flung it into the brush. Was it a game? She repeated the same thing several times, each time staying closer.

Finally, she placed a crumb in the palm of her hand and held it out. The doken flew over, taking the crumb and tossing it aside. Miran reached out and stroked its glossy feathers. "You're so pretty."

The bird wasn't looking for affection or food. It was interested in something else. It peered at the potion and pendant, stretching its head out toward them. Miran instinctively clasped her hands around both. The bird squawked, bobbing its head up and down, taking an aggressive stance, ruffling its wings.

"What are you after?" Miran asked, "What could you possibly want with these?"

The doken gently touched Miran's hand with its beak, indicating it wanted her to move her fingers away. Miran stepped backward, stumbling over a rock. Startled by the sudden movement, the doken crouched down and then flew off, vanishing into the treetops.

Carnivorous Vines

The next morning began with misty rain. After a quick breakfast of elf cakes and elf berry tea, they went on their way again, trudging along the wet trail. The thick canopy of foliage sheltered them from the droplets for a time, but then the rain fell harder, penetrating through their clothing.

After a few hours, they came—soaked and shivering—to the end of the trees. The drizzle was starting to relent, the suns straining to break through the clouds. They regarded the strange landscape before them; the ground was covered with close-knit rocks that spiked up in triangular formations, a narrow carpet of greenery winding in between them, creating mossy pathways.

As they ventured onward, the clouds cleared and they welcomed the warmth. As they continued on, the path became more difficult to traverse. The density of the rocks increased, the green path becoming thinner and thinner until there was only an expanse of stone before them.

At the end of this stone expanse was a wall. It was tall and covered in vines, constructed with rectangular and square rocks, stretching as far as the eye could see in both directions.

Findy scratched his head. "This is as far as I've ever been from home, it is. I don't know how to get around this wall."

"Can we fly over it?" Astrielle asked.

Miran looked up and around, then behind them. "Galloping on this stone floor could split the camions' hooves."

"There must be an opening somewhere," said Satrah.

They dispersed, pressing on different parts of the wall, feeling for weak spots. Findy discovered a stone that had gaps all around it and was loose. "Over here!" he called. "I think I found it, I did!"

Pushing away the vines revealed a red larimar stone embedded in the loose brick. Rays shot out from stone, connecting with Miran's fiery pendant. A warm sensation burned on Miran's chest. She looked down to see that the stone in her necklace was luminous and hot to the touch. Both stones began to pulsate to the same rhythm until the beams increased to an intensity that accelerated to a blinding flash.

"Ooooh, look," said Astrielle.

"It's glowing," Satrah said.

The loose block in the wall moved away with a grating sound, stone against stone. When it had cleared the back of the wall, it slid to the side. The surrounding stones did the same in succession until there was a void large enough to pass through.

"Let's go!" said Miran.

As soon as everyone was the other side, the stones slid back into place of their own accord.

They had entered a new world. Lustrous, vibrant green hills teeming with colorful flowering plants studded the horizon, with gently flowing rivers tracing glorious patterns along the valley floor. The air was perfectly calm and the suns soothingly warm. Butterflies flitted from one exquisite bloom to another. Dragonflies darted over the lakes and streams and colorful birds of a multitude of varieties preened themselves, serenading each other with spectacular melodies.

Satrah was mesmerized. "This is the most beautiful place I've ever seen," she said, her voice velvety smooth.

"Ooooh," giggled Astrielle softly. "Soooo pretty."

Miran wasn't so sure about it. "Keep your eyes open. This may be too good to be true."

"Indeed, it is." agreed Findy.

As they walked along, the luxurious grass beneath them receded, giving way to vines stippled with sharp thorns that scratched the camions' legs. Beast whimpered from the sharp pokes in his paws and the blue doken flew overhead, cawing more loudly than ever, like a warning bell.

The vines on the ground began flowering spontaneously, their golden blossoms becoming so dense it was impossible to avoid trampling them. As they were stepped on, a fine amber colored vapor rose up, winding its way around the air. The vapor gave off an acidic aroma.

Astrielle waved a hand over her face. "What *is* that *smell*?"

Findy yawned and pointed. "It's coming out of these flowers, it is."

Miran yawned, laziness overtaking her. She looked up at the cawing doken. Something was wrong. "We need to move more quickly," she said. "That vapor is poisoning us." She felt so tired that she could hardly move one foot in front of the other.

Satrah was in a daze, a big grin on her face. "Can't we stay here just a little while…longer?"

Miran tried to lead them away, but every step made the vapor thicker and more pungent. "Let's go back," she said weakly. "Find another way."

Astrielle rubbed her eyes and relaxed onto Cavalo's head, curling up into a ball. "I'm so sleepy."

Satrah fell to her knees. "I'm going to lay down for a bit."

"No!" Miran said. "Quickly, everyone, cover your faces." She pulled a corner of her cloak over her nose, fighting the urge to close her eyes.

Astrielle looked at Miran, her eyes half shut. "Get on Cavalo and fly," she whispered.

166

Miran saw that Astrielle's mouth was moving but she couldn't make out the words. It was a slow chirp in the distance, devoid of meaning. Dizziness enveloping her, she rested her head against Cavalo and closed her eyes. When she opened them again, she saw her companions in various states of collapse as her legs buckled beneath her. She sank down, her head heavy.

The camions growled and nipped at the thorns and vines which were traveling in an upward spiral around their hooves and legs.

Astrielle cried out, "Miran! Look!"

A tiger mouse scurried by and one of the flowers flicked out its tongue, catching the rodent with the stickiness, then pulled the writhing creature into its mouth.

Vines were everywhere now, sliding up and around like ravenous snakes. Miran felt drugged. She had made it this far, she just *had* to get to the summit. She opened her mouth to speak, but it refused to make any sound, as if it had been stuffed with cloth. "Use your daggers," she mumbled, her voice a hoarse whisper.

More and more flowers were opening, baring their sharp teeth and wagging their gluey tongues. The victims fought lethargy and chopped weakly at the stalks. When a vine was cut, a sizzle escaped from the blossom. Grey liquid oozed out of it, then the petals blackened and shriveled up.

The doken plunged repeatedly, using its beak to damage the climbing vines. Satrah received a painful bite on her leg from one of the blossoms just before she severed its stem. Miran, Satrah and Findy struggled to cut the vines away, and as they did, the vapor lessened, giving them a chance to breathe fresher air and clear their heads.

With effort, Satrah and Miran mounted their camions and Findy lumbered onto Beast. With little time to escape before the vines began another round of attacks, they galloped away from the carnivorous vines and lifted into the air, heading toward the summit.

No Turning Back

Flying high above Saron, they had a clear view of the magnificent mountains rising in the distance. Below, smooth, flowing rivers wound in blue satin ribbons from the tops of the mountains down to the rocky cliffs that towered over the vast sea.

A flock of grey birds overtook them, passing by in a noisy blur. Then, suddenly, there it was—the treasure trove of coveted jewels atop a cylindrical rock formation—millions of crimson stones shooting out blinding red beams. Mixing with the sky and the clouds, the beams created a sky of purple brilliance.

A narrow strip of land surrounded a hedge, the sides of the summit dropping at a ninety-degree angle. A dome-shaped translucent forcefield topped the summit.

Astrielle clasped her hands together, her mouth opening wide. "Ohhhh, it's more beautiful than I could ever have imagined!"

"Do you think we can penetrate that dome?" Satrah wondered.

Miran spotted an area on the perimeter that looked large enough. She tilted her head toward it. "I'm not sure. Let's set up camp on that patch of land and find a way in from there."

"Looks good, it does." Findy said.

Miran aimed Cavalo toward the summit and they made their descent.

As they set up camp for the night, Satrah's attention was drawn to a rhythmic sound coming from the hedge. "I hear something," she said. "Coming from over there. I'm going to take a look."

"Be careful," Astrielle warned. "You don't know what it could be."

Miran said, "She's right."

"I'll be fine," Satrah said, going toward the hedge. Upon close inspection, she discovered that it was covered with white buds and the buds were snoring.

She touched the force field behind the hedge with the tip of her sword and it undulated like water, the waves rippling outward. This seemed to disturb the buds and they opened, revealing tiny flower faces. They yawned, all of them moving in perfect unison.

"Come quick!" Satrah called out to the others.

Miran, Findy and Astrielle gathered around as the flowers spoke in a whispering, high-pitched timbre, all together. "Who aaare yoooooou?" their collective voices echoed across the valley.

"I am Miran from the Island of Zarada and these are my friends."

170

"She's going to be the next Sultana," added Astrielle.

"Oooooooohhhh. The next Sultanaaaaaa," cooed the buds.

"How do we get into the red larimar field?" Satrah asked.

Their tiny mouths opened, their faces were struck with terror. "Nooooooooo, you must not go in. The daemons will kiiiillll yooooooouuu."

"There must be a way in," Miran insisted.

"But no way ooooooouuuut," the buds countered.

"We have to enter," said Miran. "The future of Zarada depends on it."

"You must fiiiiiiind the statuuuuue."

"Where is this statue?" asked Findy. "It would take days to travel the perimeter searching for it, it would."

Miran said, "We don't have days."

The flowers grew sleepy. "Taaaakes tooooo looooong," they purred.

"Hey, wake up!" said Satrah, nudging the force field again with the sword. "Tell us how to get in!"

"We will sleeep noooow," said the flowers. "When weee waaaake, you will be deeeeaaad."

"But what about the statue?" asked Miran.

"Go north. When the full mooooooooons shiiiiiiine high in the skyyyyy, at midnight, you may enterrrr."

The flowers fell back into slumber, their millions of little eyes shutting tight, and the snoring commenced.

171

"That's tonight, it is," said Findy, gazing up at the sky, which was already darkening.

Miran drove the last stake into a corner of her tent. The sky was freckled by a plethora of stars and dimpled by two rising full moons. "Let's all get some rest. In a couple of hours, I'll go find the entrance."

"Let me go," Satrah volunteered. "I'm not tired. I'll find the opening while you rest."

Miran hesitated. "I don't know. It might not be safe."

"I'll be fine, and I promise to be back to wake you before midnight."

The look on Satrah's face was so full of eagerness and sincerity, Miran couldn't deny her. "All right," she agreed. "But please, be careful."

"Yes, it's dangerous," Astrielle warned.

"I didn't know I was bringing two mothers on this trip," Satrah said.

Miran and Astrielle laughed.

"And a father!" Findy added. "Those daemons are tricksters."

"I'll be okay," Satrah reassured them as she took Otho along the perimeter, the edge of the summit crumbling just beyond her footsteps. She walked for some time with no sign of the statue. Fatigued, she wiped the sweat from her forehead and took a swig of water from her flask. She began to wonder if she should turn back, then she noticed a dark shape up ahead. Drawing closer, she realized it was the statue. It was a giant replica of Miran's pendant—the Rain Goddess. The moons were obscured by clouds, but she could see it well enough. She gazed up, admiring its grandeur and elegance, marveling at the enormity of the larimar stone at its heart.

The wind pushed the clouds away and when the moons shone full on the statue, their light encased the larimar stone and the statue began to vibrate. Red beams of light radiated outward from the stone's center. Then, in a moment, the statue evaporated, leaving a gaping hole.

Satrah peered down into the hole. Before she could stop it, a strong force pulled her down. She grabbed onto Otho's legs, shouting, "Pull me back!" But Otho wasn't strong enough either. Unable to resist, they were both sucked into the hole and pulled under the hedge. They emerged on the other side, right in the middle of the red larimar field.

Facing the Daemons

Glaring in displeasure at the dirt, Otho shook out her fur and began licking herself clean. Satrah brushed off the dust and took in her surroundings. It was quiet and still, the air damp and cool. The huge expanse of silvery plants, each one sprouting luminous red gems, shimmered in the moonlight, the stones ranging from the size of a thumb to the circumference of a melon.

She touched one lightly, her fingertips taking on a red hue. Closing her fingers around it, she gripped it tightly and pulled, but it wouldn't budge. She yanked it hard and still it refused to be separated from the stalk. Raising her dagger, she pulled the stalk taut and brought the blade down hard, severing it.

A shrill sound emanated from the plant when it was cut and the daemons, in their nearby lair, were alerted by it. The sound meant the presence of an intruder tampering with their precious stones. In an instant, several daemons went out, their wispy forms drifting toward the field like white ghosts.

Satrah slid her dagger back into its sheath. Now that it was no longer attached to the plant, the stone

174

slipped easily out of the stem. She slid it into her pocket and led Otho back to the wall, eager to show the others what she had found—if she could figure out how to get back.

As she moved toward the wall, she heard a strange sound fading in from overhead—a soft flapping. She looked up to see a bunch of pale figures coming right at her.

The daemons were made of pale white shreds. They had the ability to change direction in a split second with their vague shapes of heads, torsos and limbs. Traveling briskly to Satrah, they were eager to reclaim their heisted gem.

Satrah attempted to jump back into the hole. But the force going the other way was too strong. She saw no other way out. Perhaps it was possible fly up and break through the force field, but she couldn't be sure. Mounting her camion, she broke into a hard gallop. But the daemons reached her before she could get away.

Satrah screamed as she was pulled into the night sky by one daemon while another plucked the stone out of her pocket. She turned her sword to the "kill" setting and managed to pierce the third daemon, turning it into a puff of smoke that dissipated into nothing. At the mercy of the daemons, she was escorted to the lair.

Into the Lair They Go

A screeching sound startled Miran from her sleep. "What was that?" She sat up.

Findy had heard it, too. "It must be the stones. They alert the daemons when they are cut, they do. I didn't realize she would..."

Miran cried, "Satrah! I shouldn't have let her go!"

Astrielle shrieked, "Oh, no!"

Miran jumped out of her sleeping bag and climbed onto Cavalo.

"Miran, take us with you," urged Astrielle.

"You shouldn't go alone," added Findy. "You shouldn't."

"It's too dangerous for the both of you," Miran insisted. "I don't want anyone else risking their life for me."

"But you are risking yours for us," Astrielle astutely pointed out.

"Very clever, my friend, but I still say no. This is my quest and my risk to take." She began walking. "I'll be back by moon down...with the stones..."

Findy and Astrielle held the same thought in their minds; fairies and elves couldn't be expected to just sit around and wait when a friend needed them. They had only to look at each other and a spark of understanding passed between them. Findy tilted his head, twinkling his eyes at Astrielle. "Shall we?"

Astrielle's face lit up. "We most certainly shall!"

In a blink of an eye Astrielle had settled onto Beast's head, where she had a clear view of the path. Findy mounted Beast and they trotted as fast as his little legs could take them. After they had gone on for some time, Astrielle began to worry. "Ohhhh," she fretted. "I don't see her anywhere."

Findy tried not to let the fear get to him. "She's up ahead, she is. We'll find her."

Astrielle tried her best not to succumb to fear, but it was no use fighting it; she was petrified. Spooked by the tiniest insect chirp and smallest rustle of leaves, ducking at every shadow and gasping at every misstep, she was a bundle of nerves. "Oh!" she cried, when Beast tripped, revealing a sobering view of the drop.

"You can't let the fear getcha!" Findy said, pulling the reigns to the left with one hand while grabbing hold of a thick vine with the other. They had almost plummeted to their deaths.

Astrielle's voice was shaky. "Just be careful. If we fall, I can fly, but you and Beast...well, he needs a running start, and—" She didn't want to finish the sentence.

"I know, I know," chuckled Findy. "I'll be like a squashed bug, I will."

"How can you joke about it?"

"That's what elves do when they're nervous."

"Oh, I see."

"Shhh," he whispered. "There she is."

In the light of the moon, Miran stood before the statue, her face tilted up toward the Rain Goddess, tears glistening in her eyes.

Findy's eyes widened. "It's just like…"

Astrielle put her finger to her lips. "Shhh! I know!"

Where Are the Saronians?

The daemons' lair was fashioned out of misshapen grey rocks and had become riddled with mold and fungus over time. It was a dismal and dark structure, invariably cold and damp. Diffused light filtered in through all the cracks and crevices and the suns provided enough light and warmth to make the environment visible. But it was not habitable for warm-blooded beings like fairies, warriors or elves.

Ethereal beings from another dimension, daemons were not exactly alive. They didn't mind the lack of light and weren't bothered by the sticky drops of moisture that oozed down from the low ceilings. They had no noses with which to smell the putrid odors that seeped up from the stagnant moisture pooling and festering in the puddles on the floor. In fact, they were sensitive to too much light. Full exposure to the suns disintegrated their delicate forms, burning them away.

The underground caves and the network of mazes connecting them had been constructed by the Saronians in ancient times. At that time, various rooms were used to sort and store harvested stones, the trade and sale of

179

which was their primary livelihood. The stones had a myriad of uses, from prompting rain to healing and ceremonial rituals to elaborate jewelry. The Saronians lived in dwellings near the field and spent their lives cultivating and caring for the red larimar plants—until the daemons came.

The daemons arrived one day, driving out the Saronians, who fled to the mountains. Some claimed that they lived there still, in the far reaches of the wilderness, but no one had seen them since they left the summit long ago.

The daemons were heartless, mindless creatures who neglected the field, allowing it to grow wild. They did nothing to stop the invasion of weeds and choking vines that threatened the health of the plants. Anyone who wanted stones had to sneak in and outwit them in order to take what they needed—or die trying. Many of these fell victim to the daemons, losing their lives.

At one time the High Council considered sending warriors to the summit to oust the daemons. But they couldn't get a majority vote and the Sultana was not keen on the idea. So, they were reluctant thieves.

Satrah was taken to the main room and forced into a metal chair. "What are you doing? Let me go!" She was surprised at the strength these beings possessed. It wasn't muscular brawn, but some kind of energetic power they were wielding over her.

Her wrists and ankles were bound and her forehead strapped to the back of the chair, restricting movement.

A daemon carrying a long thin black tapered wire came toward her. She struggled against the bindings that cut into her skin. "What are you doing?" she cried. "Stop!"

The daemon gave no indication that it heard her plea. It only drew closer, setting the sharp tip of the wire against her cheek. Satrah cried out as the daemon applied pressure, piercing her skin, and pushed the wire into the side of her face.

Satrah felt no pain as the wire entered her cheek and reemerged just below her eye. The color drained from her face. The poison in the wire made her throat thick and her skin turned a sickly shade of green. She tried to speak, but all that came out was a faint whimper.

Anay's Journey

Anay had been directed by her mother to trust no one, so she traveled without any companions and kept to herself. Taking the sea route secretly determined by Selexi, she enjoyed the smoothest journey to Saron, experiencing clear skies and calm waters all the way. She slept soundly, ate heartily and landed on the opposite side of Saron without a scratch.

Selexi had gotten her this far, but how she was to get herself to the summit remained uncertain. She would have to figure that out on her own.

She disembarked and began the trek, using the map as her guide. Her side of Saron was dry and hot. Expanses of dirt stretched out for miles ahead with little shelter from the suns. When her water supply ran low, she rode her camion by night and slept by day beneath the sparse shade of tall cactus plants. She learned how to open the cactus and dig out the soft flesh, sucking the moisture out of it.

The journey turned out to be more of a challenge than she had anticipated. By the time she reached the base of the summit, she was hungry and dehydrated.

She wondered if Miran had made it. The idea that her nemesis might have arrived before her drove her on despite her fatigue.

She spotted an indentation about half-way up the summit and rode her camion up to it. Entering the mouth of what seemed to be a cave at a gallop, her camion's hoofs echoed along the cave floor. She stopped and dismounted, exploring the shadowy recesses with a small torch.

A growl emanated from the darkness beyond. In a moment a ghastly creature was hovering before her, its wings flapping vigorously. Its head was made up of purple crystals and its yellow eyes glistened. Roaring, it dove toward Anay, its teeth bared. Anay pulled out her sword, but the creature was too quick. Anay spun and kicked, but the creature backed her into a corner. Anay opened her transformational potion and drank it down, reciting a spell. She turned herself into a small flying insect with a poisonous bite and bit the creature, who collapsed on the floor.

Anay turned back into herself, moving deeper into the cave. Water dripped from the ceiling and trickled down the walls. She found a spiral staircase that went up and up. Her camion's hooves slipped on the wet moss that coated the rocky steps. At the top there was a metal grate secured with a padlock.

With a few swings of her sword, she broke the rusted lock and pushed the gate up. Leading her camion into the passageway, she entered the heart of the lair.

There was a muffled cry. She peered through a crack in the wall and saw the main room. In one corner sat a giant glass chest, overflowing with shimmering red larimar stones. A daemon tossed a stone onto the pile. On the other side sat Satrah, a wire sticking out of of her face.

So, they did get here first.

Another daemon floated toward Satrah, inserting a second wire in her other cheek. The panicked girl began to calm down, staring blankly into space, concentric circles pulsating around her eyes. Bars slowly emerged from above and below her.

Anay had been trained to protect the other warriors no matter what. She felt an impulse to save Satrah but checked herself. Her mother would never forgive her if she were to do such a rash thing. Selexi's instructions droned in her head: *Trust no one. Help no one.*

And yet—she felt an obligation to abide by the code she had sworn to when she became a young warrior. She *could* release Satrah but leave her there to figure out her own escape, then gather a bagful of stones from that chest and head back home before Miran even knew she had been there. She set her sword to *kill.*

Breaking through the wall, she charged at the daemons, killing one while the other whooshed away. The bars closing around Satrah locked into place just as Anay reached her. She slashed at them, but her sword could not bend or break them.

An alert howl resounded and a team of guards flowed in. Anay was able to slay many of them, but she was outnumbered. She was subdued and thrown into a cell.

Danger in the Daemons' Lair

Miran eased her way along the cliff's edge, staying tight against the wall, pulling Cavalo along. The edge crumbled, clods of dirt tumbling to the bottom hundreds of feet below. At last she came upon the statue. Bowing her head, she pleaded silently. *Help me find my way.*

She turned her head at the sound she recognized so well. Astrielle flew up, her wings buzzing away. Findy stood a few feet away, waving happily.

"I told you to stay at the campsite," she scolded, unable to be genuinely angry.

"We couldn't let you go alone," Astrielle chirped.

Findy patted Beast's head. "We're glad you're okay, we are."

"Thanks, but you really shouldn't have. You're putting yourselves in danger."

Astrielle shrugged. "We had to!"

"Friends stick together, they do," Findy said.

Miran looked up at the sky. "Well, since you're here you might as well come along."

The full moons were obscured by a patch of clouds drifting past. As soon as the moonlight shone full, the statue disappeared and they were pulled into the vacuum. Once on the other side, they gazed in awe at the glittering field, a dazzling wonder to behold this close up.

"Ooooh, pretty," sighed Astrielle, flying up to a large stone that glowed red on her face. "I can see my reflection in a single facet. Let's take some."

Findy's eyes gleamed with delight. "Yes, and go before they notice us, we should."

Miran shook her head. "We have to find Satrah. Then we'll get our stones." The lair loomed in the distance. "Let's go."

But before they could go very far, daemons sprung up from behind the plants.

Astrielle jumped into Miran's pocket cowering deeply.

"A bunch of ugly things, you are!" Findy said to them.

Beast growled and barked in agreement.

Pulling out her sword, Miran did her best to mask her fear. "Daemons! Take me to the lair!"

One of them spoke in a low tone. "What do you want and how many more are you?"

Miran waved her sword at the daemon. "I am Miran of Zarada and I demand you return Satrah, the warrior you have. And I wish to have ten stones to take back to the island of Zarada, so we can have rain. We are starving without it."

"Ahh," it replied. "You shall have no stones."

187

"I shall," she said.

"We have your Satrah," said the daemon in a low rasp. "She wants stones, too. So many thieves are you."

Miran held her ground. "We are not thieves. I am asking you to give them to me. And in exchange we will let you live."

The daemon snickered darkly. "Why would we give you anything? You are an intruder in our field and we need the stones to power our world."

"Surely you don't need all these stones for yourselves," Miran stated. "There are enough to share."

The daemon let out an evil howling laugh. "You will not have even one!"

And then they attacked.

Miran slashed at the flurry of white fluttering shapes. Crouching, weaving and turning, she pierced them as they came upon her. As soon as they made contact with the swirling light, their forms dissipated into smoke. Then one snuck up and grabbed her from behind, binding her with a trap.

Miran couldn't reach the daemon with her sword, the arm of the trap being longer than her own. Another daemon wrenched the sword away from her and she was lifted into the sky, Astrielle in tow. Findy and his pet were captured as well.

"The ugly things have us now, they do!" Findy cried.

Whisked away, Astrielle tucked into her cloak pocket, Miran felt anger simmering inside her. She wiggled and struck the daemon with her fists, but it was like hitting air. "Let go of me!" she demanded.

She tried to reach her potion but was impeded by the grasp of the device. Finally, she got hold of it, pulling it up and around her head, but she lost her grip and it slipped through her fingers. She watched helplessly as it sailed to the ground.

Soon they were in the daemons' lair. Rushed through a maze of slimy rooms and murky corridors lined with crooked rock walls, Miran noticed that the bottom half of the structure was underground. In the cells were tiny holes to the outside created by cracks and gaps in the rocks.

Findy and Beast were thrust into one of these cells, but Miran and Astrielle were taken to the main room. Miran saw Satrah in her hypnotized state, eyes wide and unblinking, red circles pulsating around them. Miran reached for her sword but remembered they had confiscated it.

She ran to her friend, her hands gripping the bars. "Satrah! Satrah, talk to me!"

Satrah said nothing.

Next to Satrah was an animal, one that they had seen grazing in the valley.

The leader daemon floated in.

"What have you done to her?!" Miran demanded.

"We have prepared her for our feasting," said the daemon leader. "In a few days, she will be ready."

"Ready for what?" asked Miran.

"She will release her vital energy to us," the daemon answered.

"What does that mean?" Miran demanded.

The daemon looked at Satrah. "We live off animals mostly, but they barely sustain us. When your kind comes along, we feast until we are full. We cannot store the energy, so we will take it from one of you at a time. Your animals will be our dessert."

"What happens to her after you've taken her energy?" asked Miran.

The daemon stroked Satrah's face with its ethereal finger. "She becomes one of us. Only your kind can become one of us. The animals—they simply die."

"What do you know about a warrior from Zarada who used to harvest red larimar stones?" Miran asked. "Galanee."

"Ah, yes, Galanee," the daemon recalled. "That was some time ago. She was a clever one—able to take the stones undetected somehow. Until we caught her in the act."

"When did you last see her? Did you take her— energy?"

"We almost captured her, but she got away."

The daemon suddenly lost patience. "Enough talk! It's time for us to have our meal. You can watch."

"No!" cried Miran. "Let her out of there. Now!"

The daemon, ignoring Miran's plea, howled out a rhythmic pattern that reverberated through the lair. All the daemons answered the call with the same howl as they converged in the room, huddling around the animal.

They began sucking the air in and soon sparkling blue energy trailed out from the deer's eyes and entered the bodies of the daemons by the force of their inhalations. As it swirled inside their transparent bodies, the animal shrunk down into a pile of fur and bones.

Selexi as Predator

Selexi, wearing commoner's clothing, stood at the large library window, surveying the sky, waiting for darkness to descend. As the light dwindled, the trees changed to black against the cobalt sky and she pulled the last piece of her costume—a crone's mask—over her face.

With all the hungry creatures lurking, fairies were most vulnerable at night. They were told repeatedly not to fly at night and to travel in groups during daylight. Still, many went missing each season. There were inevitably times when fairies found themselves alone at night and, knowing they were easy prey for carnivorous birds, oraks and, on occasion, larger beasts, the lone fairies took to the air with reluctance and trepidation.

Selexi always stalked fairies under the cover of night, but she had to be careful. If caught, she would face execution. Traveling deep into the forest, she hid herself behind the trunk of an ancient tree, one she had used for this purpose before.

Sometimes she went home empty handed, but tonight she was to be lucky. After about an hour, she

192

heard the buzz that indicated the approach of a hapless fairy. Then, the sight of softly glowing light. She positioned herself just so, held out her net and *swoosh*, caught the little thing, just like that. She felt the familiar tug, accompanied by the sickening whine of stuck fairy wings and then the shrill voice crying for help, which she always found dreadfully annoying.

"Be quiet, you!" she barked.

The fairy continued to howl in distress, but no one heard and no one came.

Selexi took the hostage to her laboratory, where the terrified fairy was tossed into the keru's cage.

"Kill it," Selexi said to the keru, her voice as hard as ice.

The miserable fairy crouched in the corner and sobbed as the keru approached. It gripped its hands around her delicate neck and strangled her until she was dead.

Potion's Surprise

Miran awoke to the chill floor of a dungeon cell. She shivered, the cold having penetrated her bones. Her head ached and she was sore all over but she could only think of one thing—Satrah.

Astrielle hunkered down in Miran's pocket. "This is not where we want to be. I'm going to fly and warm up." She lifted up and flew around the cell.

"No, it's not," Miran agreed. "And we won't stay here." She inspected the room; three sides were constructed out of stone, the fourth made of rusted metal bars. She ran her hands along the walls. Solid. The ceiling had what looked like a hatch, but she couldn't reach it.

Miran pointed to the ceiling. "See that hatch? Push on it, tell me how strong it is," she said.

Astrielle pushed on it. "It's not going anywhere," she said. "Not without tools or weapons."

Miran sighed. "We have to get to Satrah before they take her energy."

"What about Findy and Beast?"

"Of course. We have to find them, too." Miran pushed and pulled at the bars. They held firm. She was surprised to see the doken. It was standing just outside the cell, holding something in its beak. It fluttered toward her, squeezing itself between the bars.

Astrielle giggled, "You followed us here? Funny doken."

The doken approached Miran, offering her the transformational potion.

"Look!" Miran said. "My potion!"

"Smart doken!" Astrielle remarked, clapping her hands.

"How did you know?" she asked the strange bird. She reached out and patted its head and took the bottle. The doken cooed.

Miran walked across the cell, posing a question, "Now, what can I transform into that will give me the best chance of saving everyone and still allow me to gather stones?"

She paused for a moment, considering her options. "I know!" she said, uncapping the amulet and raising it to her lips. But the doken went wild, flapping its wings in her face, preventing her from drinking. Miran turned away and tripped on an uneven part of the floor, almost spilling the precious contents. The doken stayed close, poking at the potion with its beak.

Miran was puzzled. "What are you doing!?"

"Thirsty doken?" said Astrielle with a shrug.

The bird pressed its beak to the mouth of the amulet, attempting to access its contents.

Miran glanced from the doken to the necklace. "But why would *you* want to drink *this*? There's water all over this place." She gestured to the moisture dripping from the ceiling and the moisture on the floor.

"Maybe—" Miran said. "There's a reason it wants it."

"It can't be a good enough reason," Astrielle warned. "Don't do it."

Miran paused, wondering why she was even considering giving the potion to the doken. Something inside her, an unexplainable impulse, drove her to hold the amulet up and offer the potion to the bird.

Astrielle shrieked, "Miran! It's our only chance to get out of here alive!"

The bird tipped its head back, opening its beak.

Astrielle covered her eyes, peeking through her fingers and then shutting them again. "Oh, I can't watch," she lamented. "I'll have to go back to Zarada without you and tell them you gave your potion to a doken...oh, dear me."

The murky liquid slid down into the doken's gullet.

Miran wondered if she had just thrown away her only means of escape for the sake of a thirsty animal. She looked at Astrielle with a forlorn and beaten expression. "Well, you'll have a great story to tell."

"I'd rather have you," said Astrielle. "Oh what will become of us?"

Miran jiggled the bars again, "I wonder where Findy and Beast are."

"They must be in another cell."

"Can you find them?"

"Me?" Astrielle asked. "But what if the daemons catch me?"

"I don't think these bars are going to budge," Miran said, despairing. "You'll have to be brave now."

Astrielle gasped. The bird was shaking uncontrollably. "Oh! It's dying. The potion did it. It was all for nothing. Oh, dear."

"Poor thing," Miran said, going to the bird and stroking its feathers.

The bird went slack and fell to its side, its wings splaying out. Then it convulsed and shuddered, morphing from one thing into another. Emitting unintelligible sounds, it grew larger and larger with each new form, until the potion had completed its work and all was stillness.

"Oooh," Astrielle said, shocked by what she saw. She blinked twice, not believing her eyes. "A Zaradian?"

"Impossible," Miran said.

An elderly woman with white hair sat before them. She held up her hands and studied them, then touched her face. She smiled in relief.

Miran removed her cloak and put it around the shoulders of the stranger who looked at Miran with immense pleasure. "At last!" she croaked. "You liberated me! I knew you would."

Miran's face lit up; old emotions came flooding back as her burden of grief fell away. "Mabu? Is that you?"

"Yes, my dear. It is I."

"Mabu!" Miran threw her arms around Galanee, tears of joy flooding her eyes.

"Hello, fairy friend," Galanee said to Astrielle over Miran's shoulder.

Astrielle flew around the cell. "*That's* why you kept pecking at the potion," she chirped. "I didn't realize you were that bird. I'm so sorry I tried to keep you from drinking. That wasn't very nice of me."

"It's all right," Galanee said. "How were you to know?"

From the other side of the wall came the sound of boots shuffling across the floor. Miran climbed up onto the built-in stone bench and peered through a small hole covered in a crisscross of wires. She recognized the boots. "Anay, is that you?"

"Of course, it's me. Who else would it be?"

Miran turned back to Galanee. "It's Anay. We're here together—in a way."

Galanee's eyes sparkled with wisdom. "You're bound together in more ways than you realize."

"What do you mean?"

"You will find out in due time."

Miran turned back to Anay. "Are you okay?"

198

Anay turned away. "What do you care?"

"We might die in here," Miran said.

"*I* won't be dying," Anay retorted. "But it would make my task easier if *you* did."

Miran was stung by the hurtful words. "You'd leave me behind if you had the choice?"

Anay scoffed. "This is a quest, remember? We're *competing* against each other. I can't help you and you can't help me. I'm going to get out of this cell and escape. Then I'll grab some stones and go home. You can figure out your own plan, if you're clever enough. So yes—you're on your own."

Remembering

A daemon floated over the tops of the prison cells, unlocking and opening the ceiling hatches, lowering a tray into each cell. They had to keep the prisoners alive, but the "food" they served was unrecognizable—a kind of mush. Miran and her grandmother watched in disgust as their trays hit the floor. Neither could bring themselves to eat.

"Astrielle," Galanee said, "Go find Findy and Beast. Then see if Satrah is in the chair and check if the circles are still moving around her eyes. After that, come back and tell us what you saw."

Astrielle wasn't so sure she was up for that. "I want to help, but—?"

"Stay in the shadows and they won't even notice you," Galanee said. "You're too tiny to perk their interest anyway."

Astrielle mustered her courage. "I suppose I'm the only one who *can* do it."

"That's right," Miran reassured her. "And you're too quick for the daemons besides."

"True!" Astrielle realized. "Of course, I'll go," she continued. "You know I would do anything for you." And she zoomed away.

"You've changed," Galanee said to Miran.

"Have I?"

Galanee pulled the cloak tighter around her body. "My clairvoyant powers were especially acute while I was a doken, but I couldn't see clearly enough to see how grown up you've become."

"I thought you were dead."

"Well, as you can see, I'm very much alive and I plan on living a good long time. Long enough to see your coronation and my great grandchildren."

"But, I…"

"You what?"

Miran spoke quietly. "I don't understand Anay."

"What don't you understand, my butterfly?"

Miran faltered. "I don't know. It's just that…"

"Yes?" encouraged her grandmother. "You can tell me."

Miran lowered her voice to a whisper. "I don't want to be Sultana…and Anay does. Part of me wants to let her have it."

Galanee took Miran's hand. "My dear, that will sort itself out. Right now, we need to focus on getting out of here—before the daemons have their way with us."

"You know a way out?" Miran asked.

Galanee grinned, her eyes twinkling. "I know these daemons pretty well by now. I outsmarted them more than once in my time."

Miran's eyes twinkled back. "I'm so glad you're here. But what about Anay?"

"What about her?"

Miran thought for a moment. "I can't leave her here."

"Good girl. Tell her."

Miran hesitated.

"Hurry," Galanee urged. "We're running out of time."

Miran climbed back on the bench. "Anay," she began.

Anay was sitting on the ground, her back against the wall. "What do you want?"

"You won't be able to do it alone…get out of this place, I mean. I can help you. I *will* help you."

Anay's eyes shifted. "I don't trust you. You'll betray me as soon as I give you the chance."

"I won't. I promise."

Anay stood up, stretching her legs. "Who were you talking to?"

"My grandmother," Miran replied.

"Really? She was here on Saron all along? Why didn't she return to Zarada?"

"It's a long story. But the important thing is that she knows how to escape."

"Why is she still stuck here then?"

202

"She transformed into a doken and couldn't transform back."

Anay ground the toe of her boot into a crevice in the floor. "Well, it doesn't matter. I don't need you. Or her."

Miran persisted. "But we can beat the daemons if we work together."

Anay smirked, shaking her head. "You're just trying to trick me so you can use my abilities to help you escape. Then you'll leave me here to rot."

Miran felt her neck grow hot with anger, and the words poured out before she could stop them. "You sound just like your mother. I always wanted to be friends with you. She's the one who pulled us apart. Haven't you figured that out by now?"

"You know we can never be friends," Anay sneered. "*Ever.*"

Miran felt old resentments churning in her heart. Tears, sharp as a river of needles, pushed their way up, but she kept them down. "I'm sorry I was born first. I'm sorry I love Grideon. I'm sorry…about…everything." All she wanted at that moment was to be back home in her cottage, with her family.

Anay stifled the feelings flooding the dam of her emotions. As much as she pretended otherwise, she cherished the times she and Miran had played together when they were small. Before she understood that she was supposed to hate Miran, she would sneak away to meet her. They would meet in the forest, exploring the world of their imaginations. They were too young then to comprehend why Selexi was keeping them apart. All they knew was their mothers didn't get along, and vowed in their innocence to be friends forever, no matter what. They sealed their pact by interlacing their fingers together.

When they grew old enough to start Warrior Training, Selexi became increasingly strict with Anay, just as the other girls were gaining more independence. Selexi insisted on knowing where Anay was at all times, always finding reasons to keep her from spending time with the other girls.

Anay stayed civil to Miran as long as she could, but over time Selexi's influence overtook her own ideas and her desire to be obedient to her mother eclipsed everything else. Selexi convinced Anay that Miran had in fact stolen her right to rule and as the coronation drew closer, the blade of Selexi's bitterness sharpened. In this way Anay learned to be just as bitter and angry as her mother. And yet...and yet—there were times when Anay experienced moments of confusion and this was one of them. Somewhere deep inside she still loved Miran.

She shook the memories away. *That was long ago...things are different now.*

Miran slid her fingers through the wires. "It's not your fault your mother turned you against me. And it's not my fault I was born first."

Anay looked up at Miran's outstretched fingers. Her mother suddenly seemed very far away, unable to come to her aid. She had to think for herself and make her own decisions. *I will take the offer if it benefits me, but I will help no one.* She stepped up and laced her fingers through Miran's.

"I found them!" Astrielle's voice called.

"Miran!" Galanee called.

"I'll let you know the plan," Miran told Anay quickly before she pulled her hand away and jumped down to the cell floor.

Astrielle was chatting away. "…Findy and Beast are just two cells down and Satrah is right where we left her, with the circles still turning. Everyone is okay!"

"So, now what do we do?" Miran asked.

Galanee started to explain. "First we must get the keys…"

But there wasn't time. The daemon guards descended upon them. Two roared at Galanee, growling and prodding her with a sharp stick. She was cornered in the back of the cell. Two more locked Miran in the trap and pulled her out.

"Take me instead!" Galanee cried. "Not her!"

Miran tried to resist but couldn't free herself from the grip of the trap. The door slammed shut and Galanee cursed at her own helplessness. Miran reached the back of her neck and unhooked the goddess pendant, dropping it to the floor.

Astrielle picked up the necklace and brought it to Galanee who held the charm tightly as she watched Miran being dragged away.

Escape Plan

Astrielle was poised and ready. Galanee peered through a crack in the wall, measuring the position of the suns. They were reaching their apex. "Now!" Galanee shouted.

One by one, throughout the lair, the floating daemons collapsed inward and "slept". Astrielle dashed and sped through the maze until she reached the main room. Satrah and Miran were still in a trance, spirals swirling around their eyes.

"I'm going to save you, just like you saved me," Astrielle said to Miran. "And you, too," she said to Satrah.

Locating the cabinet Galanee had told her about, she attempted to open it, but wasn't strong enough. She spotted a rock on the floor in the corner of the room. Wrapping her arms around it, she flapped her wings as hard as she could, lifting the rock and positioning it just so. She let it go and the rock hit one of the handles and the cabinet doors flew open. Pleased with her success, she retrieved the keys and whirred back to Galanee.

"Excellent," Galanee said as she unlocked her cell door. Next, she unlocked Anay's cell. Anay eyed her suspiciously.

"This is your last chance to get away!" Galanee urged as she went on to free Findy and beast.

Anay, caught between her mother's will and her own, was frozen for a moment in indecision. But before she had time to think, Galanee came back and came into her cell, grabbing her by the sleeve. Anay resisted. "How do I know you're not plotting against me?"

"You don't."

Anay went with the old woman, expecting the deception that was sure to follow.

Galanee guided them all briskly through the labyrinth, dodging the multitude of "sleeping" daemons hanging in mid-air, suspended like floating webs.

In the main room, Galanee used one of the keys on the ring to unlock the bars around the chairs. As they opened, she rummaged around in cabinets and drawers. At last she found what she was looking for—Anay's potion.

"Hey, that's mine!" Anay protested.

"This is the price you are paying for your freedom," Galanee said as she pulled out the wires and forced some potion first into Satrah's mouth, then into Miran's. The pulsating around their eyes faded as their eyes focused.

"Findy, remove Satrah's bindings. I'll do Miran's," Galanee instructed.

"I can do that, I can," Findy said.

Anay reached into the chest, pulling out stones and shoving them in her pocket, but Galanee warned her, "Leave them. They are not potent anymore, they've been separated from the stalks too long." Galanee located some old clothes and put them on.

Anay rolled her eyes and threw the stones back into the chest.

Miran got up from the chair.

"Are you okay?" Galanee asked Miran and Satrah.

"I think so," Miran said.

"Who are you?" Satrah asked Galanee, standing up.

"They'll be awake soon!" Galanee urged. "Grab your swords and let's get out of here!"

Miran coughed. "It's Mabu!" she told Satrah as they picked up their swords and slipped them into their belts.

"Mabu?" Satrah asked. "You were right, she's alive!"

They headed through the labyrinth, Miran stumbling through the damp maze, fighting dizziness. She hoped that Anay being with them meant things between them would be different now.

Galanee raced toward a beam of sunlight shining beneath a doorframe up ahead. But when she tried it, the door was locked.

"Anay, you and Miran are the only ones with enough strength to open it," Galanee said.

Anay and Miran used one of their warrior kicks at the same time and the door broke open.

"We're free!" Astrielle sang.

"Let's go!" Galanee shouted.

Coming out into daylight, they squinted through the brightness. Their camions grazed in the corner of a grassy area.

"Cavalo!" Miran shouted, running to him.

They mounted their animals, Galanee riding on Cavalo with Miran. Galloping past the red larimar plants, they ascended into the crimson colored air, the stones glowing and sparkling like a thousand red stars projecting a million beams of light below them. Galanee stole a glance behind. It was only a matter of time before the pursuit would begin.

Inside the lair, the daemons expanded out of their trance. Discovering the prisoners gone, they let out alert howls. Squads of them rose up from the lair.

This was the time of day that had full sun exposure. The daemons wouldn't last long outdoors—the heat would burn them away in a matter of minutes. Only if they were fast enough could they catch up with the young warriors. They had to hurry.

The young warriors fought the daemons off, slicing through hundreds of them with their swords, vaporizing them into nothing. And still more came. As they neared the perimeter, Galanee shouted, "Dive!" It was their opportunity to harvest stones.

With the daemons on their heels, only inches away, Anay and Miran swooped down into the field, slicing off red larimar stones in bunches.

Galanee directed them to rise steeply and soar upwards, toward the translucent dome. "Hold your breath!" Galanee advised as they burst through the forcefield. Emerging on the other side, they were relieved to find themselves unscathed other than the damp layer of film that stuck to their skin and clothing.

The daemons, unable to penetrate the forcefield, howled in defeat. Those that had stayed out too long met their bitter end, disintegrating into puffs of vapor, swept away by the breeze.

Miran and Anay led the group on a freedom flight over the trees and mountains, fresh red larimar stones bursting from their satchels, the bright jewels painting a trail of red across the brilliant blue sky.

Landing in the valley beyond the creeping vines and the rock floor, they walked late into the night, finally arriving at the elf village around midnight. The elf Chief and his wife, thrilled to see Galanee, welcomed them all with a celebration banquet. Fires were stoked and elf cakes were roasted around the open flames. All the elves came to admire the shimmering stones and congratulate the warriors.

In the wee hours, the sleepy elves padded away to their homes. Astrielle was settled into Miran's pocket, having fallen asleep to the sound of crackling wood.

Galanee asked Miran and Anay to stay at the fire with her before they went off to their sleeping bags.

Anay hadn't spoken a word since they had left the lair and Miran was beginning to wonder if her hope of reunion had been wishful thinking.

"Will you tell me now?" Miran said to Galanee. "Why were you unable to come back home to us?"

"Yes, yes, I will tell you," Galanee said. She stared off into the distance, her memory stirring. "It was a routine trip to Saron, just like all the others. I had harvested the stones undetected so many times before, I thought nothing of my comings and goings anymore. I became careless.

"You see, the daemons enter a dormant state when the suns are at a certain position in the sky. I think it's a kind of rejuvenation for them. That particular day I didn't check the sky properly. I miscalculated the timing. By the time they came falling out of the sky to get me, I barely had time to take a swallow of potion.

"I drank it down before they reached me, transforming into a doken and escaping their clutches. But the potion was stale. It allowed me to become a doken, but there wasn't enough potency in it to change me back again. After I remained in that form for two whole days, I realized I was never going to change back."

Galanee looked at Miran. "I have thought of you every day since then, wondering how you were growing up, angry to be trapped in that feathered body, unable to reach you and your mother, and Freya."

"Oh, Mabu. How awful that must have been."

Galanee gazed at her granddaughter with all the love she had. "We're together now," she said. "That's all that matters."

Anay sat in stony silence, her muscles tight, her face rigid. "Is that the end of the story because I'm done listening to this drivel."

Galanee's attention shifted to the flames, her wise face glowing in the dancing firelight. Taking a deep breath, she said, "There's always more to the story. And it involves the two of you." She paused, thinking of how to say what was on her mind. "Both of you have a responsibility to resolve this conflict for the benefit of Zarada as well as for yourselves."

Miran poked the embers with a long branch. "What can we do?"

Anay felt the urge to bolt. Self-preservation was all she could think of. "I should sit on the throne, just like I was meant to. Everyone knows you don't want to be Sultana, and I'm clearly more capable."

"I don't know," Miran said. "Your mother—"

Anay cut her off. "Leave my mother out of it! She has nothing to do with it."

"Really?" Miran asked. "I thought she had everything to do with it."

Anay scoffed. "Seems simple enough to me. Give up your claim and we can be done with it. I won't even

213

ask you to give Grideon to me. You can have him all to yourself and live the simple life you're used to." Satisfied with herself, she looked at Galanee and said, "There. Resolved."

Miran didn't like what Anay had insinuated. "Grideon isn't an object for me to give or take. He has his own feelings and preferences."

"Either way," Anay said. "It doesn't matter. All I want is to be Sultana. It's all I've ever wanted. And you can give it to me if you're so interested in being my friend. That's the only way it can happen."

Miran still had her doubts. "Your mother would have too much power if I let you be Sultana. I don't trust her to do what's best for our people. Even if I have faith in you, I don't think you could keep her under control."

Anay threw a twig into the flames. "She's just an eccentric scientist with big ideas that will never come to pass. She's harmless."

Miran pulled her feet in, wrapping her arms around her knees. "Harmless enough to send us on this dangerous quest where we almost died."

"*She* didn't send us. The High Council did. Actually, it was my grandmother who suggested it."

Galanee rose and circled around the fire. "You know you two are not so different. In fact, you have something very important in common. It happened long ago, before you were born, and your mothers might not

214

want me to tell you, but I believe you're old enough to know the truth."

Miran and Anay glanced at one another. What didn't they know?

"Your mothers were in love with the same man."

"So, what if they were?" asked Anay, feigning disinterest.

Galanee continued. "Brodein was married to Selexi, but he didn't love her. He only married her because she was the Sultana's daughter and his parents had arranged the marriage to bring the two families together. He really loved Adean. That makes you sisters—half-sisters."

Miran shook her head. "That can't be. My mother would've told me."

"You're lying," Anay said. "You thought you could fool me? Make me bend my position? Well, it didn't work."

Miran looked at Anay with fresh eyes. "But if it *is* true, then—"

"But it's not true," Anay said. "And you know it. Both of you are in on this."

Galanee had no patience for Anay's insolence. "You are a great warrior, Anay, and would make a worthy Sultana. But your mother's heart is not pure. If you become Sultana, life on Zarada will deteriorate. Miran has to fight for the title. It is you, Anay, who should give up any claim to the throne."

The bit of warmth that had been shared between the girls cooled to an icy silence. This was bigger than either of them. It was clear to Miran now. Even if she didn't want to be Sultana, she had to try, for her people.

Anay could not imagine giving up on her dream, not when she had come so far. She had to win the title that was supposed to have been her birthright to begin with. She had always wanted to be Sultana, but more importantly, it was the only part of her life where she had her mother's support. The only source of attention she got from Selexi was through this one ambition. It was the only common thread between them. If she didn't have this, she'd have nothing.

Anay had suffered a moment of weakness in the daemon's lair, when her survival had been at stake. She had allowed herself to be carried away by old memories—the sweetness of their early friendship. But now she remembered the real reason she was here—to win the challenge.

Her thinking crystalized. She saw enemies in the faces of Miran and this old hag claiming to be her grandmother. *Liars—the both of them.* She didn't have to remain in the company of these imposters another moment. Her mother would be furious to find out it had gotten this far. She imagined what she would say now: *secure the throne. Kill them both.* She leapt to her feet, snatching up Miran's bag of stones.

Miran reached for the bag, but Anay pulled it just out of reach, taunting her. "You don't deserve these, you know," her voice jabbed. "You're just a common nothing and always will be less than me in everything you do."

Galanee gasped, "Anay! You're wrong. Stop!"

Anay did not relent. "You're just lucky this old loon came along to save you."

Miran held her ground. "Save *us* you mean."

"That *was* convenient for me, but I would have found a way out without her. And now, I don't need either of you spoiling my quest or threatening my rightful ascent to the throne." She threw Miran's bag of stones far off into the bushes. Pulling out her sword and moving the lever to the kill setting, she lunged for Miran, aiming to finish her off then and there.

Miran's warrior instincts kicked in. She dropped and rolled to the right, then sprung deftly to her feet, pulling out her sword.

Anay did a somersault. When she came out of it, her hair was covered in dirt and leaves, her eyes wild and vicious. "All right, let's fight for it!"

The girls circled one another, their blades glowing brightly against the night.

"No," Galanee implored. "Not this way. We must return to Zarada. You will fight it out there. In front of the High Council."

"We don't need them," Anay sneered. "They've interfered enough."

"If one of us is killed," Miran said, "the other will be disqualified and put to hard labor. Neither of us will become Sultana."

Anay circled her rival. "Where did you get that notion? Or is it just another lie you're making up as you go along?"

"Your mother told me. She wanted to make sure I didn't get any ideas. Of course, I never know if *she's* telling the truth or not."

Anay hesitated. "Fine," she spat, seething. "You'll never make it back to Zarada anyway." Walking backward, she lowered her sword and pointed a finger at Miran. "You are not my sister." Then she turned to Galanee. "And you are not my grandmother."

Galanee's eyes glinted in the firelight. "That's what happens when you live a life built on lies. You never can recognize the truth when it's staring you right in the face. You can't even be sure when *you're* telling the truth."

Anay smirked. "What do you know about it? You know nothing about me!" And with that, she turned and disappeared into the obscurity of the shadows.

Miran, her hopes deflated, sunk to her knees, feeling more tired than she'd ever felt before. The fire was dying down, reducing to glowing coals while the stars burned cold in the obsidian sky.

Homecoming

The horn blasted and Anay's ship pulled away from Saron.

Yesterday she had been an only child with one father. Now, she had to consider the idea that she may have a sister, a different father and a mother who had kept the truth hidden from her. She stood at the stern watching the beach disappear until all she could see was an enormous quilt of blue and green, billowing goodbye.

Her perception of things had changed. The implications of the new possible picture of her life sat placidly on the surface of her mind, not yet penetrating. It was too painful to allow herself to absorb the fullness of what she had learned. If the things they said were in fact true, her world would be shattered. For now, all she could do was tolerate the suffocating potential of it all and hope it had been a bluff.

Exhausted and drained, she went below, collapsing onto her cot and tossing in restless sleep. Over the next few days, she awakened for a few meals, immediately returning to her cot to lose herself again to dreamless dozing. When the ship arrived on Zarada, she dressed in her full warrior attire, wanting to look every bit the part of the heroine. She climbed the stairs and walked out on deck. Miran's ship was approaching as well, but Anay kept her gaze pointed away from that direction. There was a bustle of activity; the captain pointing in all directions, shouting orders. The anchor dropped, sails were furled and cargo was prepared.

The gong on Zarada sounded, signaling the return of the ships. Women and men all over the island hurried out of cottages, gathering up little ones, tying the babies to their backs. Everyone wanted to see who had returned, and which girl, if any, carried the stones to feed their hungry mouths and quench their thirsty land.

The High Council members filed down to the water's edge. They had been expecting the return of the girls and were anxious to see if they had obtained stones. The Sultana had been advised to stay in her quarters, but had refused that advice, demanding to see for herself what had resulted from the quest. She sat in her carriage, Raina securing blankets around her shoulders. Even with three layers covering her, she still felt cold.

As the girls came in on the rowboats, shouts of congratulations rang out. When they stepped on shore, clapping ensued. Miran pulled out a handful of red larimar stones, raising them high for all to see. Cheering erupted in a deafening roar. Babies were lifted into the air, hats were thrown to the sky and exclamations of joy burst forth. They were saved!

Festive music started up. Miran and Anay stood before the High Council, triumphant and proud.

"Which of you have procured stones?" asked Dosha.

Both girls opened their satchels, showing their glimmering red jewels.

"Release the stones to me," Dosha said.

Miran and Anay handed their bags to Dosha and she held them up, letting the islanders see the rays of luminous, crimson light. "Our daughters have been successful! We shall have rain! We shall have crops this year! Prepare yourselves for the ceremony!"

The parched islanders cried out in happiness before dispersing back to their cottages to ready themselves.

Adean ran to Miran, bursting with pride. Freya ran beside her, welcoming her big sister with a hug.

Galanee, not wanting to steal the attention away, had waited to reveal herself. She stepped upon the shore, taking in the sight of her home, and headed up to where Miran was. Adean, sure all these years that her mother had died, shed tears of joy as she pulled Galanee into their embrace. Three generations were reunited.

"Tell me about the daemons," Freya said impatiently.

Miran laughed. "I will. You won't believe how terrifying they are."

Astrielle's eyes grew big. "They were worse than I could ever have imagined."

"You'll give Freya nightmares," Adean scolded.

"I won't get nightmares," Freya said, pouting. "Promise you'll tell me everything, Miran."

"I promise," Miran said, ruffling Freya's hair.

As they made their way up the shore, Grideon met them. Miran felt his arms encircle her waist, his cheek pressing against hers. "I knew you would bring us rain," he whispered.

Selexi, intent on dominating her daughter, pulled Anay along up the shore. Miran had come home with the stones, but her triumph was tainted. Anay would always despise her.

The Sultana observed the scene from her carriage with swelling satisfaction. The islanders would be fed. It gave her great comfort to know they would thrive after she was gone. Spotting Galanee, her eyes widened in disbelief. She beat her cane on the carriage floor, exclaiming, "Can my eyes be true? Is that Galanee? Has she returned to us at last?"

Galanee was summoned to the carriage, where she bowed to the Sultana. "Your Highness," she said. "It's good to be home."

The Sultana beamed. "Galanee, my dear old friend! I thought you were dead."

"In a way, I was. Miran gave me life again." Galanee noticed the Sultana's sunken cheeks and pale aura. "But you—you seem—"

The Sultana smiled. "They tell me I am dying. But this day has made me feel very much alive. Climb in and accompany me back to the castle." Her eyes sparkled. "I want to hear *everything*."

Rainmaking

The circular stage outside the temple had accumulated debris after months of disuse and they only had a few hours to prepare it for the rainmaking ceremony. The High Council delegated tasks, the Sultana calling on the help of a hundred islanders and a thousand fairies to clean and decorate.

Once it was ready, the Priestesses gathered on the stage. Two blessed the altar by chanting solemn tones in the old tongue. Another pulled ten gleaming crystals out of their stalks, polishing them with a sacred velvet cloth before carefully arranging them on a silver tray lined with citrine silk.

The suns dropped down like heavy golden lockets and the insects began to sing their night chorus. As dusk deepened into darker shades, the islanders, dressed in ceremonial clothing, came in from the village, their laughter and conversation filtering through the forest.

The stage was framed with tall pillar candles set atop black pedestals and soft pink lights encircled the perimeter of the stage. Incense sticks sent out smoky spirals that drifted up and out in white plumes. The

224

Priestesses began chanting, soft and low. The High Council took their place on the stage.

Dosha came forward. "My dear Zaradians, you have been patient and understanding during this long drought. We could have fought amongst ourselves for dwindling resources and created chasms within our community from the effort. But we stayed strong. We stayed loyal. We stayed unified. When we were thirsty, we drank less. When we were hungry, we ate less. We followed the rationing and because of our perseverance, we have survived to see this glorious day!" She raised a goblet in a toast. "Let the ceremony begin!"

The rite began with the soft beating of drums. The Head Priestess held the rainmaking staff upright, inserting the red larimar stones into a matrix pattern. With each stone's placement, a special prayer, said in the old tongue, was intoned by Magik Elder. Her voice rose above the drumming and the chanting, each added stone causing the others to shine even more brightly. When they were all in place, the stones collectively radiated a blinding crimson light.

The Priestesses led the chant and the islanders joined in, singing with devotional fervor to the higher forces, their arms rising and swaying in unison. Some said their own special prayers to the mysterious all-knowing bringer of sky water, the Rain Goddess, as Magik Elder continued her intonation.

Beams from the stones traveled outward and traveled up, creating a radiant path to the sky. A cacophony of chanting and singing filled the air as the drums beat faster and faster still and the Zaradians danced to the mesmerizing rhythm.

The chanting intensified as giant clouds rolled in, clapping their thunder. Lightning bolts danced amongst the clouds and the stones called out to the sky, creating a mighty downpour. Raindrops pelted down like glistening sky tears.

Precious beads of cool wetness kissed their faces, collected on their tongues, ran down their arms. They rejoiced, dropping to their knees in relief, dancing and spinning, clasping hands together, beating the ground with their fists, jumping about, throwing their arms around one another in ecstatic celebration. The drought was over!

Galanee's Wisdom

Adean sat at the spinning wheel weaving burnt-orange yarn in preparation for a color change in the rug she was making. She smiled at the sight of Galanee and Freya playing a game in front of the fireplace but her smile faded when she saw the withdrawn expression on Miran's face. She was staring into her cup of tea, silently oblivious to the uneven snapping of crackling logs and the melodic chiming of happy voices.

Miran hadn't been the same since her return. She had remained despondent and inconsolable. Galanee stole a glance at Adean, who was itching to say something.

Adean sighed and concentrated on her younger daughter. "Okay, Freya, time for bed."

"Oh, Mom, not yet," Freya protested. She clung to her grandmother, trying to delay the inevitable.

Adean secured a knot. "Come on, now. It's getting late."

Freya gave Galanee a last hug. "You'll never go away again, will you?"

Galanee smiled. "I'll be around for a long, long time."

Adean took Freya by the hand and led her down the hallway while Galanee cleaned up the game and placed the box on the shelf. She sat down next to Miran, whose gaze did not stray from her teacup. "I don't feel like talking right now, Mabu," she mumbled.

Galanee unhooked the goddess necklace she had been wearing since Miran had dropped it on the floor of the daemons' lair and fastened it around Miran's neck. Miran's hand moved instinctively to the pendant, her fingers feeling the familiar texture of the blood red stone that had kept her going in the darkest hours of her quest.

"I want you to have it," Galanee said.

Miran said, "I felt so close to Anay on Saron. After the way we escaped together, I thought we would be—"

Galanee nodded. "Friends."

"Yes."

"Sometimes friends are disguised as enemies. They love you, but don't agree with you. That's a conflict many of us struggle with from time to time."

"Anay isn't struggling."

"That's where you're wrong. We caught a glimpse of the part of herself that yearns for the light of truth. Yet her shadow side is still very strong. We shall see which one ultimately prevails. If *you* stay in the light, there's a chance she'll be pulled into it."

Miran looked up at Galanee, her face awash in confusion. "How can I fight someone I love?"

"With your heart wide open, your mind resolute, and your sword drawn in strength."

The Challenges

Dosha banged the gong. "Both Anay and Miran made it back alive, each procuring the required ten stones."

The High Council had called a meeting to address the unprecedented situation. Decisions had to be made, and quickly.

"I understand they worked together to escape the daemons," said the Sultana.

Selexi interjected. "So, you see? Without Anay, Miran would never have made it out alive."

The Sultana pinched her lips together. Sometimes it was better not to engage.

Dosha nodded to Bajo, who read from the law book. "If the challenged and the challenger both complete the quest successfully, they will enter a training period followed by competitions in three categories: Magik Arts, Academic Aptitude and Physical Mastery. Their skills will be judged by the High Council in the form of points, their marks will be tallied and the young warrior who earns the highest score will be crowned the next Sultana."

"Because of their familial relationship with the contestant," Dosha said, "the Sultana and Selexi will be exempt from judging. They will be replaced with citizens chosen by the High Council."

"Ridiculous," Selexi said under her breath.

"Bring in the girls," directed the Sultana.

Miran and Anay were led in and Dosha addressed them. "You have succeeded in your quest for the red larimar stones, saving our island from drought and famine. For that we are eternally grateful. Your bravery shall be written in our *Great Book of History,* but neither of you is as of yet the winner."

She looked at Anay. "Do you still wish to challenge Miran as the next Sultana?"

Anay glanced at her grandmother, ambivalence gnawing at her. *Why am I suddenly doubting this?* But when she met Selexi's gaze, all her doubts were quelled. Her mother still had total authority over her, and she believed she could beat Miran. "Yes, I still wish to challenge Miran."

"And you, Miran," asked the Sultana. "Do you still wish to defend your birthright?"

Miran hesitated. *This is my chance to hand over the throne to Anay right now and be done with it. I can live a quiet life with Grideon. Would he resent my choice? Would Mother and Mabu understand? What do I really want? Does what I really want even matter? I have to*

231

do what's best for my people. If I know what's right, why is it so hard to decide?

She opened her mouth and let the words tumble out, "I wish to defend my birthright."

Dosha, relieved, proclaimed, "So be it!"

"So be it!" echoed the High Council.

Their destiny was sealed. They would fight for the throne. The mallet banged against the gong, cutting through the air with irreversible finality.

Miran was escorted to the castle, entering a world from which she would never return. She marveled at the size and grandeur of the place. It had been built by Sultana Undua, many years before. The wide hallways were lined on one side with sweeping windows that overlooked the Trothe mountain range. On the other side there were many doors leading to halls and meeting rooms and chambers of all sorts.

She was led deeper into the castle. At last she was stopped in front of a tall wooden door flanked by two guards. Carved into the door was the emblem of justice; two scales in the shape of female warriors. The door was unlocked and held open.

She stepped inside and the door closed behind her, the lock turning with a click. The first thing she noticed was a desk in the corner, supplied with paper and writing utensils. In the center of the far wall was a four-poster bed with a canopy of lavender chiffon lace. Violet silk ribbons spiraled up the four poles and the bed itself was covered with a richly quilted indigo coverlet. Matching velvet throws were arranged in a pattern where the pillows were.

She went to the window, admiring the majesty of the mountain range that split Zarada in two. *Just like Anay and me*, she thought; *two girls separated by a mountain of differences, trying to claim the same future.*

Magik Arts Training

Miran's eyes fluttered open at the sound of a gentle knock. It took her a few moments to remember where she was. Getting out of bed, she wrapped a robe around herself.

The lock turned and the door opened. Two figures entered: an attendant who delivered a tray of breakfast and a studious-looking woman holding a notebook.

She studied her visitor, dressed in a grey tunic and black pants. The woman adjusted her glasses. "My name is Gardova. I will be managing your schedule. During your seclusion you will have no private communications and no visitors. You may send and receive written messages to and from your family, but I am required to screen them."

Miran scooped a spoonful of sugar granules into her tea and stirred. "I understand."

"You will have three intensive training sessions in Magik Arts, Academic Aptitude and Physical Mastery. When the training is complete, you and Anay will compete against each other in each category. Do you have any questions?"

"None that you can answer," Miran said wryly.

"I'll leave a copy of your schedule on the desk here."

After Gardova left, Miran noticed that some clothes she had never seen before had been laid out for her. When had they been put there? Who had come and gone while she slept? *My life is no longer my own.*

Before the quest, she had been a young warrior, spending her free time as she wished. She remembered entire days riding Cavalo, roaming the island, visiting with Grideon and friends.

Thoughts of home and her old life made her feel jittery. *Where is Cavalo now and who is caring for him? Is Mother okay without me? Of course, she is; she has Galanee and Freya.*

She quieted her mind with a morning meditation, then nibbled at breakfast as she wrote several letters. At midday she was taken to the Magik Training School, which was housed inside the Academy. A class was in session, the apprentices gathered around stations supplied with various materials, including magik stones, colorful liquids and shimmering powders. The students held their beginner wands in position, trying to learn spells and conjure manifestations.

There were chants and gestures for each manifestation; one wrong movement or intonation and the results could be disastrous. Laughter came from one table. An accidental manifestation had resulted in a bondo with a flower growing out of its head. The image was weak and faded quickly.

Magik Elder Adiglia motioned to Anay and Miran to follow her. "Both of you have learned basic magik as part of your Academy training," she said as they walked away from the students and toward the wand keeper. "But the Sultana must be accomplished in more advanced magik, and so I have been instructed to enlighten you in the subtle magik arts and prepare you for your Magik Arts Challenge."

She asked the wand keeper to retrieve two advanced wands from the cupboard. "These wands are more powerful than the ones you're used to," she said, handing them over. "They're reserved for advanced apprentices who will eventually become Supreme Magicians. However, neither of you will be able to keep a wand of this kind—unless you become Sultana. They must be left at the school. Is that clear?"

Magik Elder continued. "Are you both heavy with the understanding that magik is sacred and must be used strictly for the ultimate good?"

"What if your idea of 'good' is different from mine?" Anay asked.

"Then you will not succeed as Sultana. The High Council will eventually vote you out and replace you with one who does share the same definition of 'good' as the rest of us."

"But my mother says…"

"Silence!" commanded Magik Elder. "Your mother is not competing for the throne. *You* are. What she says has no relevance here."

Anay refrained from saying anything more, but she was impatient with this part of the challenge. She didn't think it was necessary. All she wanted was to get to the physical part of the competition. That was where she would shine the brightest.

Adiglia led them into an adjacent room and instructed them to stand behind two pedestals. She sat in a cross-legged position, eyes closed, hands resting on her knees, one palm facing up, the other hand holding a wand. Bowing her head, she chanted. Her wand glowed yellow. She levitated, intoning, "Let us begin."

Magik was difficult. Intense focus was required in order to align with the correct frequencies. Magik Elder opened her eyes. "Manifest a vessel."

The girls said spells and waved their wands in patterns. Miran created a wide glass bowl colored translucent blue with white streaks. Anay produced a bronze urn with a green lip that fanned out to a thin rim.

Magik Elder nodded her approval. "Now pour fertile soil into your vessel."

Soil streamed forth from out of nowhere, descending cleanly into the pots.

"Miran, plant the seed of a gronala. Anay, a drile."

Flower seeds dropped into the soil.

"Now, grow your flowers."

Anay began chanting and soon a drile stem sprung up and from it bloomed a stunning large flower with vibrant orange petals.

Miran's mind was clouded, her hands shaking. She tried to produce a gronala but couldn't invoke the spell properly. The words jumbled out awkwardly. Anay snickered. Miran's flower finally sprouted upward and blossomed, anemic and pale.

Adiglia frowned. "Once you know the spell, confidence is key. Without it, you can never perfect the art of magik!"

They continued with a comprehensive two-hour training session, learning more advanced techniques of magik. Miran consistantly fell short while Anay produced strong, vivid manifestations.

Back in her room at the castle, Miran's mind was riddled with doubt. *Am I capable of defending my right to the throne? Anay is so sure of herself and so good at everything. I am going to lose.*

She climbed into bed but couldn't sleep, instead tossing under the satin sheets. The glow of the moons pierced through gaps between the curtains, lining her worried face in white bands. When sleep finally found her, she dreamt of running through a dark wood, unable to find her way home.

Warrior Training

Madeek and Anay leapt around each other in complicated acrobatics, silver shards of pink light cutting through the air in rapid sparks. Miran stood at the door, waiting her turn.

Out of all the races in the realm, the warriors of Zarada were the most skilled in battle. The Zaradian men were the greatest weapon makers on the planet of Xud and so their young warriors had the best warring implements to train with.

The Zaradians were, paradoxically, also the most peaceful society, fighting only when necessary. They were often called upon to defend weaker neighbors who didn't have the means to fight off intruders. This was a rare occurrence—those who were not allied with the Zaradians thought twice about attacking those who were. And Madeek made sure they continued training in order to maintain this distinction.

Madeek gave the signal and Anay stilled her sword.

"Anay, you may go." Madeek said.

Anay passed Miran in stony silence.

Madeek looked at Miran and said, "Drink up, then choose your weapons."

Miran picked up the goblet and drank the "traveling" elixir that would allow her to mind travel during Supreme Warrior training, ensuring she would not be hurt during dangerous maneuvers.

She chose a long, slender sword, two daggers, and a shield. She had never sparred with Madeek before and was uneasy about the prospect. Anay seemed to have had no trouble keeping up with the legendary Warrior Elder, but that wasn't a surprise. Anay was highly skilled.

Miran had never put much effort into her warrior training, never really valuing the importance of it. Lack of confidence gnawed at her. "Why haven't we done this before—at the Academy?" Miran asked.

Madeek readied her weapons. "This is something you would have done in your nineteenth year. The Sultana has decreed that you and Anay are to accelerate your training in order to prepare for the competition."

The elixir was taking effect. Miran's head felt light, her body weightless. She lost her balance for a moment before adjusting to the new sensations. Sliding the daggers into her belt, she kept the sword in her right hand, the shield in her left.

Madeek focused inward. "Close your eyes. Breathe deeply. Tune to my vibration. Connect with my energy stream. That's it. I have you. Now, follow me. Here we go!"

Miran's body grew flexible, mutable, taking on the consistency of liquid. She became flowing consciousness pouring into a vacuum of light, shooting through time and space through a vortex of stars and moons and planets. Her eyes were still closed, but she saw Madeek in her mind's eye, up ahead. All around her, the vast universe expanded outward in all directions, spiraling endless and dark, shimmering heavenly bodies shining like jewels.

They sped toward one of the planets, and when they reached it, everything stopped abruptly. Miran opened her eyes. She was back in her body, but knew it was not truly her body. It was an illusion. Her real body was back on Zarada.

In front of her was a field of tall grasses and towering trees, the air layered with fog. The sky was swathed in shades of grey and muted purple. The ground beneath her feet was a thick layer of damp rust colored leaves, dead and decomposing. In the distance, jagged grey mountains rose up, bare and severe, protruding from the dreary landscape, their tall peaks disappearing into the clouds in search of the suns.

Madeek stood a few feet away. Miran braced herself as her teacher jumped high, flipping over Miran and landing behind her. The young warrior reached back and used Madeek's shoulders as a hinge to flip over her. Madeek upped the ante by slicing her left arm around to strike, but Miran was ready. She caught Madeek's arm in midair and twisted it backwards, using

241

her strength to pull Madeek around. Madeek leveraged her body weight to force Miran to the ground. Miran kicked, but it was too late—Madeek had her pinned.

Miran cried out, then suddenly found herself alone; her teacher evaporated. She made her way across the field, looking all around, wondering where the strike would come from. And then it happened—Madeek pounced on her from behind. Miran wriggled away, running to a tree and climbing it quickly. Madeek bounded after her and when she had almost reached the top of the tree, Miran jumped down and ran away.

Madeek dropped from her perch and caught up with Miran, backing her into a corner between two tall rocks that butted up against one another. She pressed the blade of her sword against Miran's neck with one hand and squeezed Miran's wrist with the other. Miran's sword fell. She didn't have the strength to push Madeek away. She was trapped.

Madeek released her. "We try again," she said. Miran rolled into the bushes, hiding. She didn't even see it coming. Madeek swooped down, grabbing Miran and lifting her into the air. Miran kicked Madeek in the face and Madeek released her. Miran fell to the ground, suddenly finding the whole exercise pointless. She ran away laughing. "Try to catch me!" she sang playfully.

Madeek was not pleased. "Miran! This is not a game!"

She chased after her.

Miran leaped over fallen trees and skipped around boulders until she came to a cliff. A massive canyon stretched out below. It would be so easy to just step off the edge…

Madeek had had enough foolishness. Surging forward, she gripped Miran in an arm lock and bent her backwards over the edge of the cliff. If she let go, Miran would drop. Even though they were in an altered reality, Miran's body back on Zarada could suffer from the trauma of the perceived impact. The fall could kill her. Instead of having a sobering effect, however, it only fueled Miran's amusement.

Madeek was furious at the blatant disrespect of their purpose. "Shall I let you go?"

Miran's laughter faded into apathy. "Maybe I would end up in a better place."

"What could be better than being our next Sultana?"

Miran looked away, pain lining her face. "Maybe I'd rather be free."

Madeek pulled Miran back from the edge and let her go. "If I could, I would put the fierceness in you, because that's what it's going to take to win this challenge. But I can't put it there. I can't win it for you." She pounded her fist against her solar plexus. "It must come from here." Then to her heart. "And here."

Madeek gazed beyond the canyon. "Some, like Anay, are born warriors, but she doesn't understand the Zaradian way. A true Zaradian knows when to fight and when to lay down arms. She and her mother are fighting all the time. You are the opposite. You don't know when to fight. But know this—*now* is the moment for you to fight with everything you have."

"I don't know if I can."

"There's only one way to find out."

Madeek's form folded into itself. Miran felt herself being pulled with her, back through the vortex of stars and space and consciousness until they were back at the Academy. For the next two hours, Madeek put Miran through her paces in a hand-to-hand combat session.

Exhausted and sullen in her thoughts, Miran stumbled outside and boarded the carriage. The training was over and Anay had outdone her once again. The next day the competitions would begin. Madeek was right; she didn't have the fierceness she needed to win. But it was difficult to care about any of it anymore—she felt defeated already.

Magik and Academics

The islanders took their seats in the stadium and the air buzzed with excited conversation. Cheering and clapping broke out as Miran and Anay strode into the arena dressed in the attire of Supreme Magicians: tight black pants reinforced at the knee, red tunics with the symbol of a silver star, tall grey boots and a cape.

A white circle had been drawn on the ground. They stepped into it, facing the High Council. Magik Elder Adiglia floated above the ground. "You will begin by performing, on command, a series of high skill manifestations. Now, take your positions and ready your wands."

Miran and Anay went to either side of the circle where the black pedestals stood. They lifted their wands and waited.

Adiglia began, "Miran, manifest a froke!"

Miran concentrated, trying to keep her wand steady. Murmuring the incantation, she waved the wand just so and a small froke appeared, a blue amphibious creature that lived in swamps. It croaked loudly and the crowd laughed.

Miran exhaled in relief and looked to Magik Elder for approval, but Adiglia was no longer there. Her voice bellowed from behind, "Anay! Manifest a torg."

Anay focused, chanting a series of phrases in the old tongue. With a wave of her wand, a warty torg appeared. It also croaked then faded away. The crowd was thoroughly entertained.

Adiglia called out a variety of objects, one after the other, each one coming and going faster than the last. Magik Elder pointed to Miran. "A bondo!" Then to Anay, "A snat!"

Creatures of all kinds and objects of all sorts faded in and out, appearing from nowhere then disappearing into the ether from whence they came. She increased the tempo, pushing the limits, causing multiple objects to manifest simultaneously, overlapping one another.

On and on she went. "A rock! A stick! A bracelet! A boot!" The girls worked feverishly to keep up with the pace.

And then suddenly it all stopped. Adiglia retreated into the ranks of the High Council and they gathered up their scores. Miran had done better than she ever had, but Anay's manifestations had still been better—larger, healthier looking and clearer to the eye. The High Council added up the points and Anay was declared the winner. She raised her arms in victory and the islanders applauded.

Later that day, Miran and Anay were taken to a classroom at the academy. A High Council member supervised them as they completed the Academic Challenge. It consisted of a comprehensive written exam covering the many subjects they studied, ending with an essay. In the evening, the results were announced; Miran was the victor. They were now tied.

The Fight for The Throne

Miran and Anay, gloriously attired in tight red and purple Supreme Warrior tunics and shimmering black leggings, made imposing figures on the stadium floor at the final competition—Physical Mastery. With weapons secured in their belts, Miran was faced with the most difficult task she had been given so far—fighting someone she both loved and feared.

Head Elder Dosha stood at the front of the platform, her robe whipping in the wind. "Today you will prove to us your physical abilities. You must stay within the circle, fighting by the rules of the Zaradian Warrior Code." She rang the gong and shouted, "Begin!" The young warriors faced one another inside the perimeter of the circle, the roar of the crowd reflecting the islanders' heightened anticipation.

Without taking her eyes off Miran, Anay crossed one hand over to the handle of her dagger and pulled it out. She jumped high, somersaulted in the air and landed in front of her opponent, who twisted to the left just as Anay took a swipe at her face. The sharp edge grazed Miran's cheek and a thin red line of blood appeared.

Miran winced in pain. There was no chance of winning this challenge—she could never match Anay's warrior prowess. All she could do was try to hold her own with a minimum of humiliation until it was over. For the sake of her family, she had to maintain her poise and defend herself as best she could, then go home. Pulling out her dagger, she felt the eyes of the islanders upon her—their scrutiny boring a hole in her confidence. She dabbed the cut with her shirt sleeve. It was just a matter of time before Anay made her victory official.

"Why don't you just give up?" Anay said, jabbing her dagger toward Miran's face, taunting her.

Miran dodged. "Because you don't deserve the throne."

Anay laughed. "No one deserves it more than me!" She flipped high and landed behind Miran, confident and smug.

This was a move Madeek had drilled her on and Miran remembered it well. The next time Anay flew in the air like that, Miran twisted around, grabbing hold of Anay's dagger wrist. Anay pulled back at Miran's wrist as she landed, putting them in a deadlock, holding one another's arm back. They simultaneously squeezed each other's wrists in the way they were taught, causing the other to drop her dagger.

Anya pulled out her sword and Miran followed suit. The blades glowed bright pink, the swirling light crackling with electricity. Like so many times at the Academy, they sparred. But this time was different. History was being made. Their swords clanked and sparked as they flipped and dodged and pushed one another to the limit of her abilities. Miran was hanging on better than she thought, surprising Anay with her endurance.

"You never fought this well in class," Anay said, dancing her sword against Miran's.

"It never meant anything in class."

"I will win, you know."

"I know you will, but I'm going to make you work for it."

Their swords locked. They pushed against each other, but neither budged. Anay wrapped her leg around the back of Miran's leg, trying to bring her down, but Miran took hold of Anay's shoulder and pulled her to the ground instead. Anay flipped over, putting Miran on her back. The force of the impact caused Miran's sword to fly from her hand and spin away, skidding across the ground. Anay held her sword poised above Miran's heart, keeping a choking grip on Miran's neck. The islanders roared.

Miran yanked at Anay's arm, trying to pry her fingers loose. Anay, savoring the attention from the crowd, extended the moment by looking up and basking in the sea of faces that must already see her as Sultana.

Sultana Henrit had been too sick to come. Selexi sat in the royal box and Anay stole a glance at her. *You see, mother, I am worthy.* Selexi beamed back at her with a maniacal grin, reveling in the moment.

Miran could barely breathe. Growing weak from lack of air, she became delirious. Her eyes closed, her mind went black and out of the darkness, voices arose:

Madeek: "You must find a reason to fight…"

Galanee: "Fight her with your heart…"

Anay: "It's not your fault you were born first … born first …born first…"

Adean: "If Selexi gets control…"

In a flash of light, a vision appeared, a glimpse into how life would be with Anay as Sultana. People were hungry and suffering. There was no joy, only misery and bleakness. Anay was cruel and Selexi was behind it all.

Miran felt a surge in her solar plexus, a bubbling up, a rush of energy, a geyser of determination. *This is not just about me. It's actually not about me at all. It's about the future of the island. This is a test of my resolve to take my place as Sultana. It is mine to claim!*

Miran opened her eyes and, in a feat of newfound strength, pushed Anay over. The crowd sprang to their feet, cheering. Anay's anger intensified. Miran stood. Anay also got to her feet, her face red with rage.

Miran retrieved her dagger and stood tall, in the strongest of warrior stances. An image of Undua flashed in her mind. She tried to imagine what Undua would

251

have done in her position. Suddenly she was ready to own her birthright and the confidence that had eluded her now shone brightly, her eyes blazing with conviction, her power apparent.

Anay was confused by this reversal. She stole a glance at her mother, whose icy glare emboldened Anay to go in for the kill. She tried her old tricks, but Miran used her newfound inner strength to defend herself against all of Anay's tactics.

Anay was stunned. Where was the Miran she had always known—the meek and timid girl? "What do you think you're doing?" she asked.

"Claiming what's mine." Miran put her full warrior skills to use for the first time in her life. Behind her submissive exterior, she had the reserves of a Supreme Warrior. Anay was unable to keep up with the continuous barrage of attacks and ended up with her arms pinned behind her. She grimaced in pain as Miran's dagger pressed coldly against her throat.

The look on Miran's face was menacing, so much so that Anay was afraid Miran might go too far and kill her. With just a little more pressure, the blade could open a major vein and... "Please don't hurt me," Anay pleaded. "We're sisters, after all."

"Sisters!" spat Miran. "You only say that now because you need something from me—your very life! You'll say anything to save yourself."

Anay was consumed by fear, a rare sensation for her. Tears welled in the corners of her eyes.

Being a great leader entailed the use of strength. But just as important were self-control and compassion, knowing when to back away, when to show mercy. Anay, terrified of what Miran might do, struggled, gasping, "All right, you win."

"We both win," said Miran, keeping her grip tight, "I'll bring you with me, but you must denounce your mother."

Anay looked away. She could not promise anything of that nature. She would be the loser and remain enemies with her half-sister, but she would not betray her mother. "Never!" she said.

A hand closed around Miran's shoulder. "It's over," Madeek said. "You are the winner. Let her go."

Miran released her hold on Anay, who sank to her knees. Dosha declared Miran the winner and an exhilarated Miran faced the Zaradian community for the first time in full command of herself. She stood tall, her arms raised in victory, gazing up at the islanders. *My islanders,* she thought. The spectators roared in celebration.

Freya jumped up and down, exclaiming, "We're going to live in the castle!"

"Yes we are!" Grideon said as he clapped and whistled.

Adean and Galanee, bursting with pride, clasped hands.

Anay skulked away, looking around for her mother. Selexi's chair in the royal box—the box neither of them would have the right to sit in anymore—was now empty. They would be crammed into a common cottage while Miran and her family moved into the castle. She knew her mother would never succumb to that fate. So where would they go?

Henrit's Last Words

The end was near. Raina, Heggor and the fairy twins did everything they could to make the dying matriarch comfortable. They read to her and offered her warm beverages. Her pillows were fluffed and her blankets rearranged. But she was oblivious to their efforts.

Nika and Tika pulled the curtains back, allowing more light into the dark room. "This might cheer her up a bit," said Nika.

"Indeed!" agreed Tika.

The Sultana's eyes fluttered open then closed tight against the bright light. "Mother?" she mumbled weakly. "Have you come for me?"

Heggor, her face tinged with concern, examined the Sultana's life force by suspending her open palms over Henrit's solar plexus. "Tell Selexi and Anay to come quickly. She's going." Raina relayed the news to a messenger who dashed away.

Anay had come back to her room, spending a few last moments in the only home she'd ever known. She looked around the room, plagued by uncertainty. There was a knock on her door.

"Come in," she said.

The messenger entered. "The Sultana—she's—you'd better come now."

"I'll be right there."

"Your mother is not in her rooms."

"I know where she is. I'll bring her."

Once she realized Anay was defeated, Selexi hurried back to her rooms in the castle and transported all her important possessions down to the laboratory. It had been a shadowy possibility in her mind, but she hadn't quite worked out all the details in the event of failure. She never doubted her daughter's ability to win, but now it was a bitter reality.

Her thoughts were clouded by anger, raging more furiously than the experiments bubbling around her. She fumed over what had happened and, from the intensity of this anger, she schemed.

Anay made her way down the passageway, but when she knocked on the laboratory door, Selexi refused to let her in.

"Let me in," Anay said.

"What do you want, you weak, pathetic excuse for a warrior?"

Her mother's words slashed at her. "Grandmother is dying. It's time to say goodbye."

"I don't need to say anything to that miserable fool! Especially now, when everything is falling apart. All because of you, child! You have ruined us!"

Before her mother could snare her with more insults, Anay turned and ran, sprinting all the way to her grandmother's bedside. She sat on the edge of the bed, taking the Sultana's dried, wrinkled hand in hers. The dying woman's breath labored, her wizened face infused with an ashen pallor, yellow like the pages of an old book.

Her grandmother had been the only person in her life she had ever received love from. Her death, along with her mother's rejection, meant she would have no one. She folded the Sultana's hand further into hers, her heart aching with shame. Tears welled in her eyes as she realized she should have spent more time with Henrit. Regret pushed the tears out and they fled down her cheeks in salty streams.

In a vain attempt to stave off the inevitable, Raina held a cup of medicinal tea to the Sultana's lips. "No," mouthed the dying woman. "No more."

"Please drink, Sultana," Raina coaxed. "It will make you feel better."

The Sultana opened her mouth slightly, allowing some of the warm liquid to flow in, then sank back into the pillow. Raina dabbed the corners of Henrit's mouth with a cloth and placed the cup on the bedside table, her heart heavy.

Anay, hoping to receive some words of sympathy, sobbed, "Grandmother, I'm sorry. I let you down. I lost the challenge. Miran is going to be Sultana." She wept freely then, her tears making spots on the silk coverlet. "Mother will never forgive me."

The Sultana grimaced, forcing her eyes to open, a faint smile forming on her pale lips. "Good," she whispered, her eyes shining. "This is what I've been waiting for. Miran should be Sultana. That is what's right. Now I can go in peace."

Anay gasped in disbelief. "But—"

"Follow her lead," the Sultana added, her breath labored. The sparkle in her eyes dimmed and darkened and then—the light died. Anay stared at the dead woman, shocked by her words. Not even her own grandmother had wanted her to win. She was truly alone.

Preparing

The rains fell in tender droplets and in great downpours. It quenched the ground and fed the roots and life burst forth. On dry days, when the suns came out, crops were planted. The grain shoots, green and tender, waved and shimmered across the expanses of farmland. In the orchards, aromatic fruit trees blossomed, promising succulent harvests. Sea vegetables returned to their state of abundance, their tall, lush tendrils swaying in the breeze, reaching for the light above.

Animals that had taken refuge in the cool altitude of the mountain tops returned to habitats they had abandoned during the drought, multiplying once again. Beyond the valley, the hills were blanketed with millions of glorious flowers that attracted a myriad of birds and butterflies.

After the harvest and the renewal of life, everyone on the island prospered, including the bondo who rested comfortably in a bed of cool moss after feasting on an abundance of puce worms. Outside her cave, the tiger mouse mother watched as her healthy pups frolicked in the sunshine.

As decreed by island law, Miran resided in the castle for twenty-eight days prior to the coronation. Never having known this kind of solitude before, her time in seclusion wasn't easy. The luxurious room with all its amenities didn't make up for the loneliness she felt. The niceties were a good distraction but were foreign and hollow without the company of her friends and family.

She felt the limitations of her confinement, but understood it was a necessary phase of the transition. If she was going to be an effective leader, she had to develop powers of contemplation and introspection—crucial skills in making the decisions that were going to confront her in the years to come.

She had entered this period of seclusion as a child, but even in the short time period, a gradual readjustment of her perspective had taken place. She no longer fought against the restlessness she had felt so acutely when she first arrived. The urge to run to the barn, which had been overwhelming at first, had faded into an affectation of the past. Impatience had been replaced with tolerance. She now owned the space around her and moved through her new environment with quiet dignity and graceful calm.

With the guidance of her tutors, she passed the days bolstering her understanding of Zarada. In the mornings she studied detailed maps of the island—tracing the contours of the mountains, memorizing the complex system of tributaries and rivers, documenting stretches of land she didn't even know existed. She learned about the rhythms of the tides and eddies and the treasures of the tide pools. She pored over images of what seemed to be an infinite variety of flora and fauna and gained an understanding about how all living things were dependent upon one another, connected in a balanced ecology.

In the afternoons, she studied the inner workings of agriculture and the complexities of harvesting. She was enlightened about the details of the trips the men took and how much their economic stability hinged on these voyages.

She was educated in many other subjects as well, including history and politics. It was her role to continue relationships with the leaders of other communities on the planet of Xuda; she drafted her first letters to those leaders, introducing herself.

She missed her mother's voice, her grandmother's wisdom and even Freya's pestering, but life in the cottage was a world she would never inhabit again. Soon they would join her, along with Grideon and Cavalo. In the meantime, she would have to be content with her books and maps, fine clothes and sumptuous food. All these diversions, along with the kindness of those around her, helped her endure the isolation.

On the twenty-ninth day she awoke with the rising of the suns and the bang of the coronation gong. Her attendants entered, chattering with excitement. They helped her into her gown, a gorgeous flowing vision of white chiffon with tiny white beads and accented with shoes encrusted in white sequins.

In a flurry of activity, last-minute adjustments were made; a blur of needles and threads, a winding of ribbons and lace, the buffing and painting of her nails, the brushing on of luminous makeup, the arranging of her hair—braided and pinned and decorated with small white flowers.

The muffled cacophony of the crowd gathering outside the castle seeped through the windows. Miran was too lost in her own thoughts to hear either the chattering around her or the noise outside. She gazed at her reflection in the mirror as the last finishing touches were made. *Who am I now? Surely not the carefree girl traipsing through the woods on my camion. That was only weeks ago, and yet it seems like it had been someone else entirely. What will my days look like from now on? Whatever they are, I will serve as best I can. This is my destiny.*

What About Anay?

The Priestesses chanted incantations in the ancient tongue as they filled bronze bowls with sand and sticks of burning incense. Shawls were donned, scepters raised, and bells rung. Tall stakes were planted around the perimeter of the stage and wrapped with crimson and gold ribbons that fluttered and danced in the wind.

The inhabitants of Zarada were so filled with jubilation they practically skipped on their way into the arena. Clothed in a shimmering array of vibrant silks and shining satins, they were a river of colors, merging into a sea of laughter and happy repartee.

Amateur musicians played old folk songs on flutes, guitars and drums. Vendors maneuvered through the aisles, presenting food and drinks for sale. Flower wreathes were to be found upon the heads of girls of all ages. Younger children played stone and string games and chased one another, their happy voices adding to the general atmosphere of good cheer.

The mood was festive, and yet there was an undercurrent of ambivalence. They mourned the passing of their old Sultana Henrit and a sense of bittersweet feelings lingered in their hearts. Still, they were eager to welcome their new, young leader who had brought them rain. She would surely introduce new, innovative ideas while keeping the important traditions of Zarada alive.

Anay jostled through the throng, trying to ignore the sideways glances from the villagers. Now that she was no longer part of the Sultana's rule, they no longer felt the need to pretend to like her. She hadn't realized how much she and her mother were despised. But now she knew. She saw how they looked at her and understood.

I don't belong here, she realized. *But where else can I go?* There was one place she might seek solace—the laboratory. Her mother was probably still furious with her, but whatever anger was waiting couldn't be worse than being shunned by the entire Zaradian community. She jostled her way back out of the arena, going against the stream of incoming people. Out of habit, she bolted toward the castle, then she remembered—she was no longer residing there.

She and her mother had been offered Miran's old cottage, but Selexi had refused it. Anay didn't want to live there either, especially since it had been Miran's home. *Mother will let me sleep in a corner of the laboratory, next to the creatures.* Angling to the right, she raced toward the forest, where the hidden laboratory entrance was.

Crowned and Wed

"I'm ready," Miran said as she stepped forward to meet her fate—not as the nonchalant girl she had been, but as the young woman she had become—having proven her worth to herself and her people.

She climbed into a carriage decorated with white flowers and long, streaming white ribbons. It was a short ride to the arena and a few minutes later she emerged to a multitude of people, row after row, all waiting to see her crowned and wed. Every inhabitant of the island was present, including the infirm and aged. *They will look to me now to lead them. And I will*, she promised. *I will lead them as best I can.*

The Priestesses chanted, summoning a higher source. They pulled incense sticks out of sand filled pots and painted words of blessing in the air with the burning tips. The High Council sat behind the altar, solemn, still and austere. Behind them, the mountains reflected the same sentiment—stern and immutable.

Miran heard a voice behind her. "Now."

A hand gently nudged her forward. Sparkling fairies, Astrielle among them, fluttered around her, adjusting her train, sending fairy dust sailing in her wake as she walked down the aisle. Thousands of eyes settled upon her, gazing at her in adoration, Zaradian hearts beating with happiness.

One by one she climbed the steps to the platform and when she reached the top, she stood before the Priestesses and the Elders. Grideon was there, resplendent in a sapphire blue tunic and tan pants tucked into shining black boots.

Miran turned and faced the sea of people. The Priestesses continued chanting softly as Dosha held up a golden crown covered in sparkling jewels. The citizens cheered their approval as Dosha lowered it onto Miran's head. "This jeweled crown symbolizes your stewardship of Zarada. Do you accept its meaning and your responsibility to lead us?"

Miran felt the weight of the crown. "I accept."

Madeek came forward and wrapped a cape of amethyst velvet around Miran's shoulders. "This is to remind you of your inner wisdom. Will you use it well?"

"I will," Miran said.

A cool metal band was slipped onto Miran's second finger by Adiglia. "Wear this ring of the whispering wind that shows you the honorable way. Are you listening for it?"

"I am listening."

Grideon came to stand beside her. A crown was placed upon his head as well. "Will you represent the

Brotherhood and lead them in the Zaradian ways?" Dosha asked him. "Will you support your Sultana in her deeds?"

"I will represent the Brotherhood and support the Sultana," Grideon answered.

The High Priestess approached. "Miran and Grideon, we are entrusting the care of this great island to you both. Do you accept the responsibility to be our Sultana and Sultan?"

"We accept," they replied.

"Do you accept one another?"

"We accept one another," they said together.

Miran placed a ring on Grideon's finger and he placed one on hers.

The priestess concluded, "You are hereby married in the name of Zarada. May you be guided by courage, wisdom and love."

Miran turned to Grideon and he kissed her, sealing their union. The coronation and wedding ceremonies complete, it was the beginning of their new life together.

Arcodi Arrives

Chaos had replaced the usual order of Selexi's lab. The towers of books that had been neatly stacked now lay in toppled heaps. Experiments had been knocked over onto their sides and the liquids pooled and dripped over the edges of the table onto the floor.

Selexi frantically packed items she wanted to take with her, tossing anything unwanted to the side. Arcodi had arrived and was now haranguing her. "So, your precious Anay lost," she chided. "And now you need me."

Selexi suppressed her anger. "Why don't you help me instead of gloating?"

Arcodi floated to the cage that held the keru. She pulled the blanket off and leaned in to get a better look. "I'd rather look at our keru."

"Leave it alone," Selexi warned.

Arcodi smiled a hideous Vindan smile, her crooked teeth jutting this way and that. "Why are you so upset? We will produce many kerus on Vinda, away from snooping eyes, just as we planned. Then we will return to take Zarada. It's all working out perfectly." She stood to her full height. "Knowing how to make these creatures will save you from what is coming to the rest of your kind. You should be happy."

Selexi bristled at the insinuation that her fate was in Arcodi's hands. "The next step—" she began.

Arcodi cut her off. "You leave the next step to me."

"But only I know—"

Their bickering was interrupted by the sound of approaching footsteps. Selexi panicked. Had Anay given away her location? Relief overcame her when she heard Anay's special knock. But it was quickly replaced by renewed panic—her daughter meeting Arcodi could prove disastrous.

Selexi placed the cover over the cage and gestured to Arcodi to hide. She went to the door and opened it a crack. "This is not a good time. Come back later."

She tried to close the door, but before it could latch, Anay forced it wide open. "But you can't turn me away—" she said, walking into the laboratory, clinging to the folds of her mother's cloak, burying her head in Selexi's shoulder. "I did my best, I truly did."

"Clearly, your best wasn't good enough!" Selexi said, pulling away. "This isn't the time for whimpering."

"But—"

"Stop sniveling, you foolish girl!"

"I'm sorry."

"Run along now, I'm busy working."

But Anay had nowhere to go. Wiping her eyes, she gathered her composure. "What are we going to do now?"

"*We* aren't going to do anything. You ruined your chance to rule. Now, I have to continue perfecting my masterpiece. I will secure Zarada another way."

"Your masterpiece? What are you talking about?"

"It's not time yet for you to see it. It's not ready. You must leave now. I can't work properly with you here."

"But where am I to go?"

"You can live in that dreary cottage. I will let you know when it's done and then, once I finish, you can be Sultana. The sooner you leave me to it, the sooner that can happen." Selexi guided Anay to the door.

Anay looked past her mother, noticing the state of the laboratory—the boxes, the puddles, the fallen books. The only thing that wasn't askew was something she'd never seen before—something that sat on the table covered with a cloth.

Selexi tried to usher Anay out the door, but Anay would not be dismissed. Not this time. "You're not going to get rid of me," she said, moving deeper into the room. "Not before I see what *that* is."

Selexi tried to block Anay from going any further, but she was no match for her daughter's strength. Anay lunged toward the cage and in a warrior quick move, yanked the blanket off, exposing the keru. "What is this, Mother?"

270

Selexi snatched the blanket from Anay's hand, trying to put it back over the cage, but it slipped through her fingers and dropped into one of the puddles on the floor. "Nothing you need to know about." She stepped between the cage and her daughter.

Anay's sadness quickly turned to anger. "I'm not leaving until you tell me what you're up to."

Selexi's eyes darted to the corner of the room. Anay saw a flash of glinting silver. "Who's there?" Anay asked, pulling out her dagger.

Arcodi emerged. "Hello, Anay. I'm Arcodi, Dictator of Vinda."

The inhabitants of Vinda, known for their brutality, were sworn enemies of the Zaradians. "What are you doing here?" Anay asked.

Arcodi tilted her head toward Selexi, "She will tell you."

Selexi didn't like where this was going. Even in her cold heart she still had a trace of maternal instinct. She would suffer to see her child hurt. And she still had plans to put Anay on the throne and use her to placate the Zaradians. "If you must know," Selexi began, "this creature is called a keru. In large numbers, they will allow me to take over Zarada. I will build them on Vinda and, when they are ready, I will return to conquer the island."

"You mean *we*," hissed Arcodi. "*We* will build them. *We* will return and conquer. Show her how it obeys."

271

"Yes," Anay said. "I want to see that."

Selexi addressed the keru. "Awaken, keru."

The keru's eyes focused.

"Lift your right arm," Selexi said.

The creature obeyed.

"Lift your left leg."

The keru obeyed again, keeping both limbs in the air.

"Smile."

The creature mechanically lifted the corners of its mouth, revealing its small teeth.

"Jump," Anay ventured.

The keru didn't move.

Selexi said, "Sleep."

The creature went back to a neutral position.

"It obeys only me," Selexi said. "Brilliant, don't you think? My best mutant ever." She waited for Anay's praise.

But Anay was dumbstruck. "What did you mean when you said, 'take over Zarada'? How many of them are you planning to make? Exactly what will they do?"

Selexi was impatient with Anay's insolence. "Too many questions!"

Anay was not done. "But I have many more."

"You forget that I've been working all day and night in here for you—for us—so we can have our way with the future of this island. My method is almost perfected now and soon we can have everything we want—you and I and our friends on Vinda. It's not your place to question me."

"Our 'friends'? On Vinda?" Anay laughed in disbelief. "They aren't our friends. They're our enemies. How can you associate with them?"

Knowing the danger they were in, Selexi put her hand on Anay's shoulder in an attempt to calm her. "I'm sorry I didn't tell you before. Arcodi really is here to help us. Arcodi, tell her."

"Oh, yes," Arcodi said. "I am here to help you."

Anay pulled away from her mother's touch.

Selexi desperately tried to save the situation. "This is all for you; for your future. You can't turn on me when we're so close—"

Anay was repulsed, her heart sinking. "This is what you spent all your time on while you neglected me, isolated me from the other girls, sent me off to play alone? All those years wasted. For this…this…monstrosity."

Selexi's anger rose. "Selfish girl. You have no idea what *I* gave up. Much more than you, I assure you."

Arcodi seethed at Selexi, the fire in her eyes blazing bright blue. "Selexi, you'd better contain her or I'll have to take the matter into my own hands. We can't have her interfering."

Selexi knew Arcodi would kill her daughter without hesitation. But she also knew Anay was capable of killing Arcodi and then where would she be? She'd be lost. She would have no place to build the kerus. She

273

couldn't risk losing either one of them. "Please," she pleaded with her daughter. "Try and understand."

But Anay wouldn't be manipulated. "I know the truth now. Miran is my sister, right Mother? Our father loved Adean but was forced to marry you. That's why you wanted me to be Sultana, so you could have your revenge."

Selexi didn't deny it. "Adean has taken everything from me and now it's her turn to be the loser. You can still be Sultana if you work with me now. Come with us to Vinda. We will build an army to overthrow Miran for good and rule this island as it should be. I will put you on the throne where you belong."

Anay shook her head. "I always wanted to be Sultana, but not like that."

Arcodi didn't like what she was hearing. After her kind had won Zarada, there would be no Sultana, but she decided not to bring that up just now. Let Selexi build the army and invade and then she would show Selexi who was in charge. "Selexi, she knows too much."

Selexi put her hand up. "Wait. I can convince her to come—"

Arcodi roared, "It has to be done!" She shot a fireball from her eye in Anay's direction. The young warrior ducked and the burning sphere crashed against the wall, sputtering down in charred ash. The fireballs continued to fly as Anay leapt at Arcodi. Selexi jumped in between them and Anay's dagger pierced Selexi's arm.

Anay paused for a moment, locking eyes with her mother before rushing out of the room. Arcodi cruised to the doorway, following Anay, lobbing more flames. A fireball hit Anay in the back. Another grazed the top of her head and a third pelted her left leg. Arcodi went back into the lab. She could not chase after Anay and risk having her presence revealed to the Zaradians. That would surely mean her end.

Selexi followed as well, yelling, "Come back!" But it was too late. Anay was gone. With smoke and flames trailing from her hair and clothes, she sped through the darkness, toward the only person who might help her, if she could only reach her in time.

The Awakening

Grideon offered his arm to Miran and they walked together into the banquet hall. Their presence was announced, her midnight-blue gossamer gown shimmering under the soft lights. The High Council, Priestesses and other important Zaradians gathered around, bowing their heads in reverence.

A rush of warmth flowed through Miran's heart to see all who had come celebrate their coronation and a smile passed over her lips as she took her seat at the head dining table. *Yes, this is where I belong.*

A wonderful party went on for hours; musicians played festive music, sumptuous dishes were served, the guests using the finest china and stemware, brought out specially for the grand occasion. Glass vases, overflowing with fresh flowers in varying shades of white, graced the center of each table. Miran's mother sat at a nearby table with Freya and Galanee. She caught Adean's eye. It was good see her mother happy, it had been so long since they had shared a joyous moment together.

A signal was given and a parade of entertainers, dancers, acrobats and magicians streamed in. Miran and Grideon enjoyed a brilliant show. After the performance, the guests congratulated the new Sultan and Sultana one more time, wishing them well before they said their goodbyes.

After the festivities ended and the guests had departed, Miran returned to her quarters, glowing with the enjoyment of the evening, feeling happier than she could ever remember. Slipping into a silk nightgown, she collapsed into bed, immediately falling into a deep and peaceful slumber.

She had gone to bed contented, but during the night, her dreams turned dark; war and bloodshed, starvation, cottages on fire; Grideon being dragged away, her mother fighting off a hideous creature that was attacking Freya; the beating down the door of the castle and a voice proclaiming vengeance, vowing to kill her.

Miran was bolted awake by emphatic knocking and loud voices engaged in an argument. She heard a young warrior's voice demanding to see her, but the guards were refusing to let her in. Miran ran to the door and flung it open. She gasped at the sight she beheld. There stood Anay, her hair wild, her clothes blackened and riddled with gaping holes. Patches of her skin were exposed, red and blistering.

Anay stared back at Miran, her eyes wide, crazed. She struggled against the guards, but they held her arms.

"You must come. Now. Or my mother will destroy us all!"

Miran was suspicious. "Really? How do I know you're not trying to trap me into doing something that will harm me or our people?" She looked at the guards, "Take her to the dungeon."

Anay squirmed and kicked in protest as she was dragged down the hall. "Look at me!" she called back. "Arcodi did this. She is here on Zarada right now, conspiring with my mother in her secret laboratory to take control of Zarada. We must stop them!"

Miran went back into her quarters and got dressed. She tried to eat and go about her day, but she couldn't get the image of the burns on Anay's skin out of her mind. She remembered the pictures in her Academy textbook of the Vindan fireball wounds. They had a particular shape and texture, the blisters just like the ones she had just seen. There was no way Anay could have created those marks herself.

Arcodi. Here on our island without our knowledge. Secret laboratory? Could it be?

Unity

Miran and a handful of guards followed Anay to Selexi's old bedroom where the entrance to the secret passageway was; a narrow wall of stones opened when triggered by a hidden lever. Anay stepped in and Miran and the guards followed her into the passages of the castle, drenched in blackness.

The guards lit torches and Anay took them down a long staircase. "Hurry!" she called as she raced ahead. "We have to get there before they leave!"

At the bottom of the staircase was a corridor. The corridor wove this way and that, finally taking a sharp turn to the right. At the end was a large wooden door, splintered and rotting. Miran watched as Anay tried her special knock. No response.

Anay pushed on the door. It wouldn't budge.

"Break it open!" Miran ordered. The girls stepped back while the guards hacked away at the door with axes.

"Does anyone else know about this?" Miran asked.

"No one except Arcodi."

"How long has she been coming down here?"

"When she was a child, she discovered a hole in the wall of her bedroom closet. She started chipping away at it, making it larger and larger. Eventually, she squeezed through and found the corridor that led to this room."

At last the door gave way and they stepped inside. The laboratory smelled of death and damp and chemicals. Anay looked around. There was no sign of Selexi, who had taken everything of value, leaving the room fairly empty. All that was left were jumbles of overturned vessels, bunches of disconnected wires and a few unfinished experiments. What had once been a valuable collection of books had been reduced to a pile of smoldering ashes, with several corners of book covers protruding around the edges.

The mutants, casualties of Selexi's purge, were slumped over, lifeless. At the sight of their corpses, Anay collapsed to her knees, her shoulders shaking with rage and sorrow. "She killed them!" She looked at Miran despairingly. "My own mother, against us all along. Why did I never see it?"

A whimpering noise came from one of the cages. Shosi was still alive. Anay took him into her arms where he huddled and trembled in fear. "Oh, Shosi, it's okay. I'm here now." Blood trickled out of his mouth. Shosi gasped for air and then breathed no more.

"We have to stop them," Miran said. "Where do you think they went?"

Anay gently laid Shosi back in his cage. "How can you even think of trusting anything I say after how I've betrayed you? I was your enemy every step of the way. You might as well have me taken away. I'm of no use to you."

Miran laid a hand on Anay's forearm. "You see the truth now, don't you? We are sisters, you and I. Family. I will be Sultana and you will be my advisor. I want you with me always."

These words affected Anay like a dried seed receiving water and sunlight for the first time. She was being given the chance to be something better—a loyal Warrior of Zarada—what she had always wanted to be but hadn't realized it.

A latent desire sprouted within her and she suddenly saw herself in a new light, her face flashing with new purpose. Emotion overwhelmed her as words of truth came tumbling out. "They're going to Vinda where they intend to build an army of mutants called kerus. Then they're going to come back and, using this army, try to reclaim Zarada by force."

Miran commanded her guards, "Run back to the castle and assemble a search party. Search the east shore first, the side of the island closest to Vinda, then comb all other possible points of departure."

Exile

Selexi and Arcodi came slinking out of the forest and two of Arcodi's soldiers floated up and over the sand, assisting them with their cargo. Selexi's items—boxes, bags and crates, lab equipment, books and research records—went onto the decrepit Vindan boat. Casting off into the night toward Vinda, Arcodi's barren island in the northeast, they left Zarada. Very quickly, the ship was only a small spot of light on the horizon and then—blackness.

The rising moons saturated the air with an orange haze, the fine sand the only witness to a yellow night crab that crept sideways along the shadows. All was quiet, except for the rushing waves, singing up an endless chorus to an infinite verse in a boundless sky.

Zaradian guards burst out of the forest and trekked up and down the shoreline, searching for traces of Selexi. They found her footprints and evidence of items being dragged across the sand. But, looking out to sea, they saw nothing. They were too late.

Once a good distance from Zarada, Selexi checked that everything was in order. She lifted the cage that contained the keru and carried it to the bow. Smiling mischievously, she cooed, "Wake up, keru."

The keru's eyes focused and its arms moved slightly. It waited for instructions.

"You are going to give me my vengeance," she informed it.

The keru stared ahead blankly. She had designed it to have no emotions, so there would be no conflict when it came time for killing. She gazed upon its impish green face, imagining a giant army of them marching by the thousands over Zarada, bending the islanders to her will. Then she would then have what she truly desired.

She had never shared the full depth of her unrelenting, unshakable ambition with anyone, not even Anay. She had hidden behind Anay's claim to the throne, but it was always her ultimate intention to have the crown sitting securely upon her head.

And yet, she knew she may never wear the crown. The Zaradians would be more docile with Anay as Sultana while she pulled the strings from behind the scenes. This arrangement could prevent rebellion. However, Anay was proving to be difficult. Selexi had spent so many years trying to shelter her daughter from the influences of peers and teachers, but it didn't seem to have made any difference. Perhaps Anay would come around when she realized how harsh her life would be if she pitted herself against her mother.

Selexi saw all her plans unfolding clearly in her mind's eye and she shared the vision with the keru, her voice cutting like a knife, "I see it now, the entire island teaming with you and your kind smashing doors and windows, crushing skulls and splitting swords. The guards in the castle will be unable to fight you off and I will win!"

The keru remained mute and still.

Selexi went on. "And after the bloodshed is complete, the Vindans will be eliminated. Anay will beg me to take her in. Adean and Miran will bow to me. They will *all* bow to me!" A poisonous grin played across Selexi's face as she reveled in maniacal delusion, her cackle lingering long into the night.

About the Author

Michele Evans is an entertainer and award-winning speaker.

Her mission is to inspire girls to harness their inner strength and reach for their dreams.

She resides in Los Angeles.

To book a workshop or speaking engagement, send an email to: micheleevansauthor@gmail.com.

Visit www.IslandOfZarada.com to read the author's blog and learn about special events.

285